FLY GUY NEXT DOOR

Freefall, Book 2

Brandy Walker

Fly Guy Next Door, Freefall, Book Two

Copyright ©2014 Brandy Walker

Cover by Brandy Walker

Cover Image: ©Pawelsierakowski | dreamstime.com

Interior Images: CanStock Photo Inc. | leonido

Edited by Noel Varner

Beta Reader Gina Dewitt

ISBN-10: 0692233415

ISBN-13: 978-0692233412

First Print Publication June 2014

Dedication:

To Gina and Lissa. I don't know what I would have done without either of you.
Thank you for not letting me crash and burn.

Acknowledgments:

A hearty thank you goes out to badass Jumpmaster and friend Jessica Callahan.

Chapter One

Standing on the front porch waiting for her friend Steph to show up, Marlowe Scott was currently indulging in one of her favorite new pastimes. Drooling over the visual treat that was Kegen and Revlin Ferris.

They knew she was watching them. What red-blooded woman wouldn't be? They were toned, tanned, and completely and utterly scrumptious. Both sporting long, curling at the edges black hair. Glimmering dark brown eyes that, when focused on you, tried to lure you into doing something naughty. And they both had the same dragonfly infinity knot and matching intricate Celtic band tattoo.

Marlowe couldn't hold back the giggle that escaped. Twins with twin tattoos, how cute, even though absolutely nothing about them could be construed as such. She knew the meaning behind it but it still made her laugh, well...giggle really.

Rev explained they picked the dragonfly because of its speed and grace flying through the air. They identified with it when they jumped out of an airplane, experiencing the rush of the freefall dive while gliding through the air. Marlowe didn't want to inflate his or Kegen's ego more than they already were by telling them it didn't matter what design was etched into his or his twin's skin; anything would look good on them. All she said was that it was very nice. Fitting for what they did in their daily lives.

Her gaze swept over Kegen, taking in every delicious inch of him as he walked around the back of his huge black and gray truck. He was her special treat. The man she wanted more and more with each passing day.

He easily topped her five feet four frame by at least eight inches. She absolutely loved it. Tall men were her weakness. She loved exploring, tasting and teasing their towering bodies from head to toe. Something she had done the first time she got Kegen naked and tied down to her bed. He called it torture, but she knew he loved every minute of it. He moaned and bucked beneath her as she nipped at his skin before sucking or licking the offended spots.

Kegen looked her way, a sly, knowing grin kicking up one corner of his mouth. Pulling his dark blue shirt off, he used it to wipe down his lightly furred chest before stuffing the tail of it into the back pocket of his black cargo shorts. He winked at her before turning his attention back to the Tonneau cover, popping it open with ease.

Marlowe had to fan herself as heat rose over her chest, neck and face. Good gracious that man was gorgeous. The thick tattoo wrapped around his right bicep rippled as the muscles in his arms bulged and flexed. What she wouldn't give to go to him, run her hands up his arms, and feel the strength and power within. To kiss and lick the light salty taste left on his skin after a long day at work. She wanted to pull him against her body and feel how much he wanted her. Have him lift her onto the tailgate of the truck and spread her willing thighs open. Fit them together until his hard cock pressed against her needy pussy.

A shiver of excitement raced down her spine as arousal rippled through her. Her nipples puckered into tight knots. The need to head inside and masturbate warred with her need to feel his body next to hers. It was almost too much to handle. But resist she would. She didn't doubt any move on her part would feed Kegen's male pride. The knowledge that he could work her into a frenzy without even touching her would inflating that ego more.

Rev sauntered out of the house wearing similar black cargo shorts and a grey Chute Shack tank top. Too caught up in lusting after his brother, she barely noticed when he smiled and waved in her direction. His deep chuckle floated across their shared lawns, pulling her from the sexual haze she was in.

Marlowe had the decency to blush at being caught staring. That wasn't the first time she had gotten sidetracked by Kegen. It probably wouldn't be the last either. She adored him body and soul.

A sudden frown formed on her face, pulling the corners of her mouth down.

Adored him.

Now there was the understatement of the century. They had been seeing each other for a little over three months and she already adored him. What was next, loving him? Wanting to spend the rest of her life with him?

A moment's panic knotted her stomach. Her heart whispered yes while her, at times, commitment-phobic mind screamed no.

She didn't even call him her boyfriend when she talked about him, did she?

No, if she did that then it would mean he meant something more. Meant she let her guard down enough to let him in. There was no way she could be falling in love with him.

Her whimsical heart took that moment to beat out of control, contradicting the statement. Her breath caught in her throat and that giddy feeling she was experiencing all too often in his presence wrapped its arms around her and squeezed.

"Shit," she murmured in disbelief. "This can't be happening."

She thought she put the right amount of personal space between them. Enough to keep her well structured walls in place without alerting him to the fact they were there.

Marlowe had yet to meet his family, except for Rev of course. The men shared a house so in her mind that didn't count. She knew she hadn't talked about her own family. Both things she did to keep it light and casual. She felt herself wavering on her usual steadfast decisions.

She could handle meeting Kegen's older brother Quin and his girlfriend if they ever came over. But they hadn't, at least not that she had seen. The couple reconnected six or seven months ago after not seeing each other since high school ten years ago. Kegen told Marlowe, Quin was trying to make up for lost time by spending every possible moment with Laurel. From the sound of it, the plan was working. Quin was able to convince Laurel they should move in together.

As for Kegen's parents, well every time they came over, Marlowe was busy with Whispers. She didn't plan it that way but running a lingerie business, while sexy and exciting, was damn hard work.

Marlowe thought about her own parents. Kegen meeting them was a non-issue in her mind. He never asked her about them or expressed interest in knowing about them. Even if he did, her mother was no longer alive, having passed away when she was a teen and she wasn't close to her father—at all.

Rev trekked back into his house carrying two paper grocery bags, allowing her time to indulge in her lust for Kegen before Rev returned and captured his attention again. Kegen turned and leaned against the bumper of the truck. Looking in her direction, he beckoned her over with a tilt of his head.

Marlowe tightened her grip on the porch post she was leaning against. Shaking her head no, she made certain she stayed rooted to the spot, even as her body was demanding she go. Heading over to him, even for the smallest amount of time, would upend her plans for the day. She would be loath to leave him even though she knew he had to head back into work later in the day.

Kegen's brows furrowed when he canted his head to the side and seemed to study her, just as she was studying him. She tried her best not to fidget and let him know he unnerved her.

No matter how close or far away, he rattled her cage like no other man she'd known. And wasn't that a bitch to admit. Acknowledging a man had the ability to break you meant there was weakness inside or even worse; you cared for him more than you were willing to admit. She knew it was the latter in her case. Would she be able to take a step or two back before she got hurt?

Rev came back out and the guys turned their attention back to the truck and its contents. Marlowe let out the breath she didn't know she was holding as the guys became engrossed in a heated discussion.

They motioned wildly with their hands pointing in her direction, towards their own home and back at the truck. Marlowe didn't know what was being said but, from the hand gestures, she was guessing Rev was trying to get Kegen to go over to her house.

Rev finally threw his hands up in defeat before heading back inside. "You're an idiot," he called back toward his brother, walking through the front door.

She glanced at Kegen, who was now staring at her. He beckoned her over again, and again she shook her head no. He frowned and she could see him mutter under his breath. He turned back to the truck, walking around to the side to pull more bags toward the tailgate. He worked quickly and silently. Glancing up at her every few seconds as if to see if she changed her mind about going to him.

Digging her nails into the wooden post, she repeatedly told herself to stay put. She shifted from one foot to the other. The need to run to him and say she was sorry for not coming right away burned like a hole in her brain. She realized then that when it came to Kegen, she felt needy, desperate—clingy. That wasn't who she was or how she acted with a man.

Where was that strong, independent woman who decided to start a business, buy a house and live life the way she wanted? Where was her backbone when it came to this man? He was more than capable of coming to her. She didn't need to run to him at the first sign he wanted her.

Marlowe did her best to convince herself she wasn't falling in love. Attacking the one solid thing she knew.

Kegen wasn't her type—at all.

He was dependable and steadfast, the quintessential strong, silent type. He could relay everything he felt, everything he wanted with a smoldering glance and a sensual smile. He was intense and at times brooding. A man worthy of a woman who would love him for all that he was.

Rev bounded from the house, cell phone to his ear. He laughed heartily before being scolded by Kegen about needing to get shit done. Rev flipped his brother off, grabbed another brown grocery bag and casually walked back inside their house.

Why was it she couldn't have fallen for Rev? He had a grab life by the balls, free-spirited personality. If only she had taken Rev up on his offer to *rev her engine* the first time they met. He was harmless to her fragile heart; too full of mirth and mischief to ever be taken seriously. No matter what he was doing there was a grin on his face, a prank ready to be played, and a cheesy pick up line on the tip of his tongue. He had a laid back quality to him that reflected in everything he did. He was also obviously still sowing his wild oats and while she found it flattering when he hit on her, he was not the man she was looking for.

"Damn it! You weren't supposed to be looking for a man in the first place," she berated herself.

The more she thought about what she was feeling the more her stomach knotted. She didn't want her heart to get involved more than it already was. It would make her vulnerable to being hurt, to being left when he decided it was easier than working things out.

Why now? Why when things were starting to run smoothly with Whispers and in her life, did she pick the one man bound to tie her up in knots and make her fall in love? Was there any way to stop the madness before it got worse?

Marlowe sighed. No. There was no stopping the way Kegen made her feel. He made butterflies take flight in her tummy, her knees to go weak when he was near, and her heart to beat a mile a minute. He always had, right from the beginning. She looked forward to spending time with him, talking to him, and just hanging out with him. Even worse than that, deep inside where her romantic side barely breathed, she wished he would come over and say he wanted her like she was his last breath.

Marlowe let out a string of whispered curses as she dropped onto one of her porch chairs. She had been able to squash the hope of finding love for so long. Now it was flaring to life with Kegen squarely in its sight.

Kegen…the man she now knew who had the ability to decimate her.

Damn, what the hell was she going to do? Wanting a man wasn't bad, but recognizing you were falling in love with him just plain sucked ass. There were so many things that could go wrong. All of them would lead to one thing—a broken heart.

"Fuck this," she said out loud. It was a damn good thing she had other plans for the night. She needed to forget about being in love, forget about the problems this would cause, forget about Kegen for just one night. It was better to think of someone else.

She crossed one leg over the other, swinging it back and forth. Glancing at her watch she checked the time. Steph was right on schedule. Late.

Shaking her head she looked back up. Her gaze collided with Kegen's. The intensity of his stare made her body tingle in anticipation and her breath stall in her throat. She was reminded yet again that the man didn't even have to say anything and she was ready to fall at his feet. She was in serious trouble.

They stared at each other for what felt like forever, but was probably only seconds, when Marlowe had to look away. It was too intense. Feelings of need and want swamped her, clouding everything bouncing around her brain.

Stupidly she wondered what it would hurt to tell him she was falling for him way too fast and way too hard? Telling him she was scared out of her mind but wanted to know if they had a future. The worst he could say was that it was nice knowing her and they were over.

If that happened she wasn't sure what she would do. She couldn't keep living next door to him. Couldn't see him every day and know he didn't feel the same way. She would have to move—or burn his house down. Neither was a good option, though one a bit less criminal.

Thankfully, Steph pulled to a screeching stop in front of the house in her tricked out Mazda RX-7, giving Marlowe something else to focus on. The woman didn't know any speeds other than fast and out of control. It's what made them the best of friends since attending the all-girls private school together. Birds of a feather and all, her aunt used to say.

Marlowe got to her feet grinning. "Nice one, Steph," she called out as her friend got out of the car. Steph was all long limbs and tattooed skin. A short, tight black knit skirt (if you could call it that) barely covered her ass and her hot pink baby doll t-shirt clung to her impressive double-D breasts. Marlowe wasn't at all surprised she was wearing a pair of killer four-inch black heels while driving like a bat out of hell. Steph was the only woman Marlowe knew who could drive so damn well in them.

Steph's white blond hair was in a femmehawk. Puffed up on the top of her head in a kind of pompadour and flowing down her back where the pink tips skimmed the top of her ass. The sides of her head were shaved to give her, as she called it, that *badass* look like her favorite porn star Christy Mack. Marlowe didn't care how she wore it and actually thought it would help sell the lingerie from the catalogue she had planned.

A loud thud followed by a masculine grunt drew Marlowe's attention back to her neighbors. Rev looked to have dropped a big duffle bag on his feet right as Kegen slammed into his back. Both sets of eyes were glued to Steph as she sauntered up the driveway. Marlowe should have expected as much. Men were always doing dumb shit when her friend was around and it normally didn't bother her. Except this time it did. She glared at Kegen but he didn't notice. Lust and shock were etched on his face. The desire to bop him on the head surged through her body. Her hands balled into fists. Jaw clenched. The growling sound drifting to her ears…coming from her.

Steph, oblivious to Marlowe's building rage, wrapped her arms around Marlowe and squeezed before stepping back. "Hey chica. That *was* a pretty damn good stop, wasn't it? Chet is helping me with my driving skills and I couldn't resist. You live in a cul-de-sac for Christ's sake. No one is parked down here. Its perfect for coming in at full speed to see how well my baby can handle it." Steph blew a kiss to her cherry red car and Marlowe chuckled, the tension and building rage leaving her body as quickly as it appeared. Leave it to Steph to have affections for a piece of machinery.

"I'm sure my neighbors will completely understand that. They're into reckless too." Marlowe motioned to the guys who were still seemingly awestruck with Steph.

Steph turned to face the guys and did a girly little finger wave. "Hello boys," she called out in her naturally men-are-nearby, sex-filled voice. Turning to Marlowe she said, "I'm moving in! All that yummy goodness needs to be shared. Which one are you fucking and can I have the other?"

Marlowe about swallowed her tongue. "Jesus Steph," she sputtered. "We aren't just fucking."

"Oh please. Fine. Which one have you deemed good enough to date and get in your hot pink panties?"

"They're white today," Marlowe said flatly.

Steph waved off her comment. "I'm sure they're cute, tiny, and lacy. Either way, he must be a hell of a guy to get past your self-imposed chastity belt." Steph gave her a pointed look that told Marlowe she knew more was going on than what Marlowe had told her on the phone.

She didn't wait for Marlowe to deny it though. She whistled long and low. "Damn girl, I'm sorry it took me this long to get out here and see these two in person. I'm glad that job I was helping Daddy out with is finally over. No more financial forms and spreadsheets to deal with." Steph heaved an annoyed sigh. "Back to the matter at hand, which one is which?"

Steph's gaze was glued to Kegen and Rev. Marlowe understood why too. Standing together the men were a testosterone overload. Women everywhere probably swooned when the men walked into the room. Some hoping one of the guys would catch them and some because they'd never seen walking sex before.

"Rev is the one picking up the duffle and Kegen is the one evil-eyeing his brother. I'm seeing Kegen."

Marlowe looked to Steph when there was no quick, teasing reply. Steph's eyes had glazed over in a sexual haze and she was purring. "Rev." Steph said it like she was testing his name out on her tongue. Marlowe looked at Rev, who was grinning like an idiot then back to Steph. That man, for as big of a flirt as he was, would never be able to handle her. He may think he could, but Marlowe was sure he couldn't. Steph would chew him up and spit him out without a backward glance. Come to think of it, he might like that.

"I like the sound his name makes. Rolls off the tongue and would sound sexy as hell at orgasm."

Of course Steph was imagining Rev bringing her to orgasm. She had a tendency to fixate on one thing and it was difficult to get her to move on until she thought through whatever devious, dirty vision was going through her head. Marlowe, in turn, would get to hear all about Steph's torrid thoughts. "I'm sure it would," Marlowe said with a chuckle. "Maybe one day you can find out. Though I think I'd prefer you not tell me since I'm seeing his brother."

"Really? I'd want to know what the other one was like. I wonder if they fuck the same. Grunt alike. Have the same favorite position. I'll fuck Rev and you can tell me what it's like to fuck, what was his name again? Keeton?"

"Kegen." Marlowe looped her arm through Steph's and tried to turn her toward the house. "Let's go inside so the guys can finish whatever it is they were doing before you scrambled their brains."

Steph didn't let Marlowe move her. "I am starving and you did promise me cupcakes."

"Let's go then. They are ready and waiting for you."

Marlowe let go of the stubborn Steph and moved to the front door. Maybe her friend would get the hint that way. Steph looked back at the guys, a cheeky little grin playing on her face. Dread filled Marlowe's stomach. She knew that look all too well. Shit was about to go down and Marlowe might be the one left holding the bag. She could only stand there and watch what happened as though it were a train wreck about to happen.

The guys automatically locked onto Steph when she loudly cleared her throat. "Nice to finally put names to handsome, chiseled bodies," she called out. "I hope I'll be seeing a *lot* more of you now that I'm back in town." Marlowe saw Steph zero in on Rev, who had moved to the tailgate of the truck. "In fact, why don't you come *rev* my engine stud and bring that delicious looking twin brother too. Lolo can keep him entertained while I ravish you."

Marlowe's face flamed as Steph blatantly propositioned her neighbor. The woman liked sex, lots of it, however she could get it. It was a good thing the only other people out to hear Steph's words were the Ferris twins.

"Shut up, Steph." Marlowe grabbed her by the arm, yanking her inside. "Sorry about her. It's the new medication. Hormones and all that," she yelled over her shoulder before she slammed the front door. She leaned back against it, hoping the guys really wouldn't take Steph up on the opportunity to come over. "Did you really have to say that? They're my neighbors you know."

Steph was laughing as she walked into the kitchen. "You know better than to ask me that. Hey, you should put on one of those starched up business suits I know you own, push your reading glasses to the end of your nose and nibble on your lip if you're so embarrassed. Make sure you bat those beautiful brown eyes at him too. He'll forget all about me inviting his brother over for sex. I'm totes jelly ya know. All of that hot, sexy man-flesh right across your lawn. I'd be fucking both of them if I were in your position."

"Totes jelly? I don't even know what that means." Marlowe pushed off the door following after her friend. Feeling, not for the first time, that she was getting older while Steph remained young and carefree. "And I will not be role playing with him."

"Girl, I never said anything about role playing so I'm gonna take a wild guess that you two have already played Master and Secretary. You *must* be in love with him. My commitment-phobic friend would never do anything like that if she weren't. She doesn't play sexy games with men she knows she's going to be rid of sooner rather than later." Steph had found the plate of cupcakes and was in the process of shoving one into her mouth as Marlowe entered the kitchen. Steph was skinny as hell and could throw down on some food. It was something else they had in common. Throwing down on food that is.

"I am not in love with him." *Liar.* Marlowe held out her hand. "Cupcake me."

Steph pushed the plate towards her and made a knowing noise in her throat. Marlowe chose to ignore her. Steph had a point she was still trying to convince herself wasn't true.

Marlowe scowled and grabbed two more cupcakes. "Love," she scoffed. "I'll show you love." She unwrapped the cupcakes and shoved one right after the other into her mouth. She didn't know if it was to keep her mouth shut or to quiet the romantic in her from plucking daisy petals signing *he loves me, he loves me not.* Either way, Steph noticed, raised a sardonic eyebrow, and shook her head slowly from side to side.

Chapter Two

Revlin groaned out loud, garnering Kegen's attention. He smacked Rev on the back before grabbing the last bag in the truck. "You have to admit, that was a good one bro. It isn't like you haven't used a variation of it on the women whose pants you've tried to get in."

"You mean pants I've *gotten* in to," Rev retorted.

"I don't see the problem then. She sounded more than willing to accommodate you." Kegen turned away, heading into the house. His frustration about Marlowe not coming over dissipated once he saw why. All she had to do was tell him she was waiting for her friend.

Rev closed up the back of the truck with a solid bang and followed him inside.

"Of course you don't see the problem. I used that line on Marlowe the day she moved in right before you walked up, introduced yourself, and effectively made me invisible. I've been stuck in the friend zone since and now she'll never let me live it down. I bet they're in there laughing about it. They'll think I'm an idiot."

"I'm sure Marlowe already knows that. Once she tells her friend what you did that first day, if she hasn't already, they'll both think you're dumb. Karma is a bitch, bro."

"Funny," Rev said tonelessly.

"But true." Kegen put the bag on the kitchen counter and started unpacking the groceries. He couldn't help but think it was about time someone called his brother out on his behavior. Rev had been playing it fast and loose for quite a while now.

But then so had Kegen. That was until he met Marlowe. He may not have realized it then, but she was pretty fucking special.

From the get-go he was smitten. At first it was her looks.

He could admit that.

He liked the way her short, straight brown hair flirted around her shoulders. The lush bow of her lips. The cute upturn of her nose. Her small waist. Perky breasts. Luscious ass.

He liked it all.

It made his dick hard and raw need course through him. Jesus, he loved running his hands over her ribs and around her waist, feeling her delicate bones before sliding his hands down to palm her ass. He was addicted to it. So round, firm and squeezable.

He glanced at the microwave clock and wondered if he would have time to go over, drag Marlowe to the ground, and fuck the living daylights out of her before he had to head back out to the Shack for the late night skydive they were doing.

Shit, probably not. There was only an hour before he had to take off. That definitely wasn't enough time to love her properly.

Damn, he really liked her and more than just the *she's-a-hot-woman* kind of like. It didn't take him long to realize there was more than the physical attraction to her. She had confidence, in herself and in her business. She had an independent streak that made it near impossible for her to ask for help when there was something she couldn't do on her own. She was playful and intelligent. All of those things made him want to get up close and personal with her. Find out more about her. Fall a little bit more in lust with her and maybe a little bit more in love too.

The love bit—that's the part that scared him. Not as much as he thought it would, but it did. It wasn't like he thought he would never find love. He assumed he would when the time was right. His parents were still blissfully happy. Quin had finally found the one woman that completed him. They were all growing up, ready for the next stage in their lives. All except Rev, that is.

At almost twenty-eight, it was only now that he thought about his future. About finding a woman he could imagine spending the rest of his life with.

Marlowe came along quicker than he expected. Cute as could be, she didn't tease or taunt him. Play silly, immature games to try and get his attention. She was straight forward in her want of him. Easy to be with. Easy to love.

Wanting her was like an out of control freefall. It was wild and crazy and he didn't know if he was going to survive. It bordered on chaos.

The trick now was to have the one conversation that would decide his future. It sounded simple enough but he was a guy. He had no idea how to bring up something like 'where is this relationship going' and 'I'm falling in love with you' without either: a) her freaking out and thinking you're asking her to marry you, which would be fine if that was what he was going for at the moment or b) her freaking out and having her run in the opposite direction.

Kegen trudged to the pantry, arms full of canned food, when Rev stepped in front of him. "What has you lost in the clouds?"

Kegen snapped out of his fog. "Nothing," he grunted out, taking a step around his brother to finish what he was doing.

"Nothing my ass. Something is on your mind. Trying to figure if you have enough time to fuck Marlowe before we take off again?"

Rev didn't know how true that statement was. "No, I'm not. Her friend is over anyway. I don't see Marlowe telling her to sit tight while we head off to her bedroom."

Rev snorted. "I can keep her friend entertained." Rev pulled two bottles of water from the fridge, offering one to Kegen before walking out of the room.

Kegen snatched it from his brother's hand and followed Rev out into the living room. He sat down on one end of their gray L-shaped couch and nursed the drink. He would rather have a beer but drinking before jumping was not going to happen.

Rev took the other end in his usual spot; slumped down, feet propped up on the coffee table and for all intents and purposes, looked ready to fall asleep. Rev didn't say anything again until his water was empty and he elicited a contented sigh, smacking his lips in the process. Rev relaxed back into the cushions even more, closing his eyes. "I need a nap."

"I hear ya." Kegen sat back, letting his head fall back onto the cushion. Silence descended and he thought Rev had fallen asleep.

"How's it going with Marlowe? She ready to settle down or kick your ass to the curb?"

Kegen's head popped up. He found his brother studying him from beneath heavy lashes. Kegen shrugged and looked out the front window. "It's all good," he replied, keeping in mind to strike all emotion from the words.

The warm glow of the setting sun beckoned him to go outside. He loved being outdoors. Much preferred it to sitting inside discussing his relationship.

"It's good," Rev said incredulously. "That's it. Are *you* ready to kick her to the curb? You have been seeing her at least three months. That's usually when you start backing off. Is that why you didn't want to walk a couple feet to go see her?"

"Since when did you start tracking how long I've been dating a woman?" Kegen chose to ignore his brother's questions. He was far from ready to break up with Marlowe. And as to the last question, that was his own stupidity and male pride getting in the way.

"I'm not keeping track on a calendar if that's what you're thinking. It dawned on me that you haven't been together for as long as I thought. You two fit well together, makes it seem like longer. Kind of like with Quin and Laurel."

"I'm going to assume that's a good thing."

Rev shrugged in nonchalance. "It is."

"Everything is fine between us. Don't worry, she'll still be able to introduce you to her hot friends."

Rev sat up, excitement glowing in his eyes. "Good. I like Marlowe. I think she'll make an awesome sister-in-law."

Kegen's eyes opened wide. "I never said anything about that."

Rev snorted. "You didn't have to. I can see it written all over your face. You're in love."

Kegen clenched his jaw to put a halt any words that would confirm Rev was right.

Rev tried to hold out as long as possible, but he couldn't keep it in. He laughed long and hard. At one point gripping his sides, they hurt so much. The look on Kegen's face was priceless.

"What the hell are you laughing about?" Kegen growled.

"Holy crap, that's hilarious. You're fucking in love. I should call Quin so he can get in on this too."

"Fuck off!" Kegen grumbled.

Rev quit laughing, wiping the tears from his eyes, and focused back on his brother. "You won't admit it?"

"I'm not admitting shit. At least not before I talk to her," Kegen mumbled under his breath.

"You know I heard that, right? I don't see what the big deal is. So you love her. Just tell her."

Rev watched the blood drain from Kegen's face. He turned ghostly white and looked like he was going to the gallows. He didn't think talking to a woman was that bad, but what did he know.

"I don't know how," Kegen admitted, staring down at his hands. "I think she might be my forever girl," Kegen whispered out.

"Jesus, Keeg." Rev was speechless. He didn't think there were words to describe how shocked he was hearing his brother admit that. "I was just joking about the sister-in-law bit."

Kegen's lips pressed into a thin line. "You're right though. I've been thinking about spending the rest of my life with her. It doesn't scare the shit out of me like I thought it would. My only problem, well not my only one—but the main one—don't you think it's a bit early to be falling in love? We've only been going out a short while."

"It's right whenever you think it is. You can't put some arbitrary time frame on falling in love. There is no *too early*. There is a *too late* though, if you've been with the woman for a couple years and you still don't know, then you need to cut out. Falling in love happens when it's meant to be whether you're looking for it or not."

"What if she doesn't feel the same? How do I tell her without freaking her out?"

Rev shrugged. Hell if he knew. The mind of a woman was a mystery to him. "I have no idea, but I can say with a degree of confidence that when she looks at you, it's with love in her eyes. I think it's safe to say it won't go badly. Mom and Dad are going to be thrilled to have her in the family."

"Crap, mom and dad will flip." Kegen groaned and Rev couldn't help but snicker.

"Especially since she's our neighbor. What was the name of that girl back in high school? The one that had flowers delivered to the front office and you were forced to carry them all day because they wouldn't fit in your locker."

"Fuck you. This is completely different."

"Yeah, because this time you're the one head over heels in love. This is going to be epic when mom and dad find out. I'll have to make sure Quin and Laurel are here to see it all go down too. I bet Laurel will remember her name."

Stark panic clearly took hold of Kegen. His eyes rounded. He ran his hands shakily through his hair. "Maybe you can convince Marlowe to set you up with the blonde and you can do your *bed-and-bolt* act on her. Distract the family by dating her for a bit."

Rev shrugged. He really liked that idea. Not that he'd admit it to Kegen. The guy deserved to suffer a bit more at the moment though.

The slamming of a car door grabbed his attention. Both he and Kegen jumped up from the couch and went to the bay window to see what was going on.

Out front, the blonde bombshell was sitting in her car revving the engine. She let the tires squeal and burn rubber in place, the loud bass of her stereo system rattling the windows. The woman had to be going deaf listening to it like that.

Marlowe's front door slammed and seconds later she came hurrying out of the house in a tight black skirt; a low cut burgundy colored top, wicked heels and a little black purse clutched in her hand. If he didn't know better, he would think she was about to jump in the car and go partying. Kegen was going to shit a brick.

Rev's gaze slid to Kegen. His eyes were indeed bugged out, hands fisted at his sides. A slow grin lifted Rev's lips. The guy was sunk and he was just realizing it.

This. Was. Awesome!

Rev looked back at Marlowe. As a friend and future brother-in-law, he couldn't let her get in the car with that woman. Not before he secured an introduction to the hot daredevil. Rev bolted for the door with Kegen hot on his heels.

"Hey Marlowe," he called out cheerfully. "Where ya going?"

She stopped a foot away from the passenger door. Her eyes were wide and startled for a second before she relaxed. "Oh! Hey Rev. I have plans with Steph. You remember her right? Oh wait, I didn't introduce you guys." Her hand flitted toward the now still car and the passenger door popped opened. The blaring music disappeared. "Rev. Kegen. This is my best friend Steph. Steph, well, you know who they are already." Her laugh came out a little strained and he couldn't help but wonder how much the women talked about them. He hoped it was all good.

Steph leaned over taking them all in. Her tight shirt was barley holding her breasts in and he saw the gleam of interest flicker in her eyes. "What's up, stud? You going to take me up on my offer? Just to let you know, I like it hard and plenty. If you aren't up for the task, let me know now."

Rev grunted as his cock stirred behind the fly of his cargo shorts. "Oh, I'm up sweetheart. Unfortunately, I have plans for the night already." Jesus, he wished he could cancel the night jump. The woman was definitely his kind of lady and he could go for a bit of wild. It'd been some time since he'd gotten any kind of sexual workout in and she would definitely be a handful of fun.

Too bad he had other things going on, like work and making sure Kegen and Marlowe didn't screw things up.

Let's be honest, it would be best for him in the long run. Their parents would be so busy getting to know Marlowe they would forget he was single and still having a hell of a good time getting in trouble. He would be blissfully nag-free for at least a couple of months.

He looked back to Marlowe, who was still rooted to her spot; he noticed her attention was focused over his left shoulder. Rev looked back and found Kegen standing behind him. His hands were clenched into fists and heated arousal flared in his eyes. He wasn't sure if his brother was going to go caveman and drag her away or just stand there brooding.

"I remember her and her crazy driving. You know you can't get in the car with her, sweetheart. She'll probably kill you. And I'm not sure he'll be able to handle it." He hitched his thumb over his shoulder in Kegen's direction.

Marlowe's back stiffened and she stood straighter. Her brown eyes sparked with fire. "I can do whatever the hell I want, Revlin. Stephanie is a fantastic driver and would never be so reckless. As for him, I have no doubt he'll be fine."

"Like hell," Kegen growled.

Marlowe's narrowed gaze zeroed in on Kegen and she didn't look happy at all. Her mouth was in a severe frown and her forehead pinched. Rev wasn't sure he ever wanted to be on the receiving end of that glare. He didn't know what happened while she was locked in her house with Steph, but it didn't look good for his brother. Rev moved aside, inching closer to the car. He didn't want to be in the middle of this fight.

"Hey, move so I can see too," Steph demanded.

He shifted over a bit. Double-checking to see if she had a clear view, he saw she was holding up her phone. He didn't know if she was taking pictures or recording it for blackmail later. Damn, he liked this woman more and more.

Rev turned his attention back to the action in front of him. Kegen moved into the Marlowe's personal space. Instead of backing up like most women would when towered over, she stood her ground. She was practically daring Kegen to fight with her.

"You know what, Kegen Christopher Ferris? I'm mad at you right now."

"You're mad at me?" Kegen exclaimed in shock. "Now this I have to hear. What did I do to piss you off?"

"Oh please, you know."

Confusion washed over Kegen's face. Rev was feeling a bit confused too. "Apparently I don't. I've barely talked to you today. When I asked you to come over, you shook your head no and planted your feet on your front porch."

"You didn't ask me to come over. You gestured like I was some pet you could call."

"For the love of God. I didn't mean it like that and you know it." Kegen's eyes narrowed. Suspicion written all over his face. "There's more to it than that, isn't there?"

Steph snorted from inside the car. "Dude, you have no idea how right you are. She's been freaking out ever since I got here."

"Shut up, Steph," Marlowe turned her anger toward her friend. Rev didn't think she was really mad at her though. Kegen was right, something more was going on with Marlowe.

Rev's gaze bounced between Marlowe, Steph and Kegen. Steph obviously knew what the problem was, Kegen—no such luck. He was lost.

"I don't know what the fuck is going on, but you are *not* getting in that car with that mad woman. End of discussion."

Marlowe gasped and took a step back as shock washed over her face. Rev watched in fascination as she worked to clear the expression and an unwavering look of determination took its place. Clenching her jaw shut, she pinched her lips together. She took one tiny step forward. Kegen was going to have his work cut out for him. "You don't get to make that decision," she said snottily, her chin jutting out and raised a fraction. "My plans for the evening do not involve you, just as yours do not include me. I can do what I want with whomever I want tonight and any night for that matter. You have no say."

Rev couldn't help but laugh at her bravado. It wouldn't last long. He knew when his brother wanted something or someone; he didn't stop until he had it. Marlowe would find out quick enough that standing up to him like that was a complete turn on and would be punished in the most wonderful of ways.

Kegen reached out and grabbed her arm before she could move toward the open car door. He pulled her up against his body and Rev swore he could feel waves of sexual energy blast off them.

"I have more *say* than you think. I'll give you tonight Marlowe, then you and I are sitting down to have a talk. You want to go out with your girlfriends; I'm cool with that. You deserve it. You want to drink and party with your friends, call me and I'll pick you up at the bar. But you even think about picking up another man, and I will spank that fine ass of yours until it is cherry red. Remind you exactly whom you belong to. We are exclusive and I want you so damned much right now I ache with it."

She let out a gasp. Kegen cupped the back of Marlowe's head and slammed his lips onto hers. She stood stiffly in his arms a fraction of a second before softening against him. Her hands slid up and over Kegen's arms and neck until her fingers tangled in his hair. Just like Rev had seen Kegen do a thousand times before, he took advantage. He would be on a mission now that she was pliable in his arms. He would seduce her with nips, licks and soul stealing kisses. Rev had to admit he was a bit turned on by the sight. The two of them together were sheer power and beauty.

"Damn," Steph whispered loud enough for Rev to hear.

"You're telling me. I'll be surprised if he doesn't fuck her right here."

"You know she's in love with him."

"Yep," he said. "He's in love with her too."

"How long do you think it'll take for them to admit it to each other?"

Rev laughed, "Probably too long. He doesn't want to scare her away."

"I think she's afraid he'll leave her at some point. She's got some commitment issues. At least she used to when we were growing up. Ask her about her parents sometime and decide for yourself."

Marlowe and Kegen broke apart, both breathing heavily, drawing Rev and Steph's attention again.

Intrigued by Steph's revelation, Rev tucked that nugget of information away for later. He would talk to his brother about it first. Test how much Kegen knew before stepping in to what could promise to be a horrific mess. "So, things all good here?"

Marlowe glared at him. Stepping around him, she slid into the seat, slamming the door with enough force to shake the windows. Marlowe's window instantly came down. She stared mutinously out the front as Steph leaned across her and eyed him and his brother.

She looked to Marlowe then back at them and grinned like a Cheshire cat. "If you need any help just let me know. I know everything there is to know about Lolo. I know *all* of her dirty secrets." Her eyes landed on Rev as she licked her bottom lip. "You and I can get together and compare notes." She winked, Marlowe's window started going back up as the car was shifted into gear and Steph peeled out. A scream and a cackle floated in the air after them as they sped away.

Chapter Three

Steph pulled the car to a gentle stop in front of Marlowe's house as Marlowe sent up a silent prayer of thanks. Gripping the arm of the door, she attempted to steady her swaying body.

Her head felt like a bowling ball on her shoulders. Her stomach was still rolling from every turn they made on the way home. Her body was starting to hurt from bouncing around the car's interior like a ball in a pinball machine. There was nothing good about the way the evening was ending. Maybe she shouldn't have polished off that last bottle of wine. Or was it the margarita she swallowed down right before leaving Tiff's place?

Whatever it was, she shouldn't have done it.

Tiffany's *I-just-got-dumped-men-totally-suck party* was a success. If you measured it by the amount of alcohol they had consumed. It was now two in the morning, if she was reading the fuzzy glowing numbers right, and Marlowe was just hoping to make it into her house before she fell flat on her face. She didn't even care if it was in the entryway. The cool tile would feel fabulous on her overheated skin and if she got sick, well it would be easy to clean up. She just wanted inside before that happened so none of her neighbors would see what a mess she was and gossip about her behind her back.

"You gonna be okay, sweet cheeks?" Steph's head appeared in front of Marlowe's face. Her white blonde hair glowing like a halo in the streetlight.

Marlowe grasped the sides of Steph's head and rubbed her hands back and forth. "I love how soft and velvety your head feels. I think this is my favorite haircut on you."

Steph snorted. "You like the way it feels because it's turning you on. Reminds you of a man's head between your thighs worshipping your pussy, doesn't it?" Steph pried Marlowe's hands away. "That's what Sierra said when we hooked up a couple days ago."

Marlowe giggled. "Is that why she kept giving me dirty looks tonight after you said you were my designated driver?"

"Probably. She's a clingy little thing. Doesn't understand that you and I will never be anything other than friends. Too much history would be ruined."

Marlowe blinked to try and clear away the fuzzy hue of, well of everything, and turned more fully toward Steph. "Why is that? Am I not sssexy enough?" Marlowe slurred and giggled again. "Sssexy. I like the way that sounds. You're sssexy and your boobs are fantastic." She reached out to poke one of Steph's impressive breasts and had her hand slapped away.

"Girlfriend, you are toasted. You know damn well why we would never have sex and it isn't because of your appeal. I actually like having you as my best friend in the whole wide world. Falling into bed together would kill our friendship. Plus, don't you remember when we kissed back in high school? You scrunched your nose up afterwards and said you weren't a fan of boob on boob action."

"Oh yeah." Marlowe grabbed her tits and squeezed them. Her nipples puckered beneath her palms and she couldn't help but pinch the hard tips and moan in delight. "I like smashing mine up against a hard, manly chest. Like Kegen's. He always feels so hard and wonderful pressed up against these." Rubbing her knuckles over her nipples, Marlowe sighed at the memory of his warm skin.

"I'll bet he's hard every damn time he looks at you," Steph snickered. "You're fucking hot doing that." Steph pulled her hands away from her breasts and folded them in Marlowe's lap.

"God, he has a smokin' hot body. It's all manly and, just, you know, yummy." Marlowe couldn't even put into words how much she appreciated his body. *Stupid alcohol.* "You should see him when he rinses off out front after getting all hot and sweaty. Those abs and the way the water runs down them. I just want to lick him all over." Marlowe sighed again and closed her eyes. "He's like the best fantasy porn material ever."

She wasn't sure how long she was off in her erotic dreams all featuring Kegen, when her door opened up. She was so damn tired now. Her seatbelt was unhooked before strong arms wedged behind her back and under her thighs, lifting her up and out of her seat. She snuggled into the body holding her. It certainly didn't feel like Steph. The girl was strong despite how she looked, but Marlowe didn't think her friend could pick her up like that. She put her hand on the person's chest she was resting against and felt around. "Where are you boobs, Steph?"

A low masculine chuckle vibrated through her.

"Oh, a man," she murmured. "Good call. Now we won't fall."

Steph laughed, the husky sound drifting to her from behind. "My boobs are on my chest sweet cheeks. Which one is the house key?"

"Pink tip." With her eyes refusing to open to see who was carrying her, she pressed her face into his chest. Hairs tickled her nose and spicy cologne infused her senses. Sliding her hand over the guy's naked chest and up his neck, she blindly brushed her thumb lightly across his lips. They were pulled down at the corners like he was frowning. "Kegen," she breathed out and smiled. "You make my panties wet. You're so fucking sssexy."

Kegen grunted and placed a kiss on her forehead. "Good to know, Peaches."

Marlowe hummed in response. She skimmed her hand over his cheek, wrapping her fingers into his hair. "So soft."

They stopped moving and there was a rustling of bodies, followed by the snick of a door unlocking. "Okay, I'm outta here, got an early morning. Take care of her. She'll have a hell of a hangover later."

"Will not," Marlowe muttered.

"Yeah, you will, sweet cheeks. Let him take care of you. Call me if you remember."

Marlowe felt Steph's soft lips brush a kiss across her cheek. "Lips are too soft. Said that in high school too."

The door closed quietly behind her. She was finally where she had wanted to be all night long. Wrapped in Kegen's arms.

Kegen looked down at the woman he cradled in his arms. Her eyes were closed and she was breathing slowly. Her sleek, short brown hair was covering half her face. The burgundy top she was wearing was pulled tight against her breasts and slightly askew, giving him a glimpse of the curves hidden beneath the fabric. If he tilted his head down he would be able to lick the enticing skin peeking out. Her peaches and cream taste: sweet, delicious, and his favorite dessert, would explode on his tongue. His eyes roamed down her sleeping form and snagged on her scrunched up skirt. The friction of him moving inched it further, showing more of her smooth thighs as he walked through her living room.

The grip she had on his hair tightened a fraction, making him wince as she rubbed her face against his bare chest. He couldn't be mad at the slight bite of pain. She was in his arms again and, as far as he was concerned, that's where she should stay from now on. "I've got ya Peaches," he whispered into the dark house.

The light shining down onto the stove in the open kitchen also cast a soft glow through the dining room and adjoining living room. Not that Kegen needed the light to know where he was going. He'd been in her house enough to know his way around without bumping into anything.

Kegen took a left down the hall, heading toward her bedroom. He never got over the size of her bed. The heavy, wooden king size bed took up most of the room. It had a dark slatted headboard and a barely there footboard. His feet never hit the damn thing and he never felt scrunched up when he was in it. There was plenty of room to fuck her in every conceivable position without falling off. The slats provided the perfect anchor points to tie each other down.

Kegen's cock stirred thinking about the first time he let her do that. She teased him with licks and nips from one end of his body to the other, avoiding his aching dick the entire time, knowing he was dying for her to touch him there. When she was satisfied with what she had done, she took mercy on him, sliding her body down his length. Pressing her breasts around his dick, sucking on the tip before laving long licks and open-mouthed kisses along the shaft. When she sheathed him in a condom and sunk all the way down, he was certain he would come with that simple, single motion. She took her time, though. Waiting for him to catch his breath while rocking her body in tiny motions back and forth. He was helpless and subject to the most exquisite torture he had the pleasure of experiencing.

It was a good thing Marlowe hated making her bed. He wouldn't have to wrestle with the sheets or shift her around to get her beneath them. Gently laying her down on the side closest to the bathroom, he debated what to do next. "Probably need to get you out of those clothes."

Kegen knew it wouldn't be comfortable sleeping in a skirt and tight top. Carefully grabbing the hem of her shirt and pulling it up, revealing a black corset style bra with little pink ribbons holding the front together. The sight of her creamy skin pushing against the black fabric sucked the air right from his lungs. She was fucking gorgeous. He swallowed hard before pulling her arms through the sleeves and over her head.

He glanced down at the skirt that had ridden up so far he could just barely see the shiny black fabric covering her mound. He licked his lips knowing what he would find beneath: a neatly trimmed triangle above her bare lips. She loved it when he tugged on the short hair as he ate at her. Drawing a deep breath, he reached for the waistband of the skirt and began wiggling it down. She rolled onto her side facing away from him, giving him the perfect view of her naked ass. The woman was trying to kill him, he was sure of it. The tiny string of a thong bisected the perfect globes of her ass.

"Now what?" Kegen didn't want to leave. He wanted to crawl into bed with her. Feel her body wrapped around his. Wake up with her and get a much cherished morning kiss.

After that little dust up earlier, he wasn't sure it was a good idea. It was too easy to convince himself to stay though.

She wanted an evening to herself. She got it. He could stay and take care of her in case she got sick, just like Steph told him to do. It would be the perfect segue into figuring out where they were going.

Kegen saw her purse on the table by the front door. Searching through it, he found her phone and shot off a text to his brother letting him know he was staying at Marlowe's and not to worry about him.

After locking the front door and checking the garage and slider door, he headed back to Marlowe's room. Stripping down to his boxers, he climbed into bed next to her. The second he laid his head on the pillow, she wiggled until hers was pillowed on his chest and her hand wrapped around his waist. A gust of warm breath skated across his skin as Marlowe sighed contentedly in her sleep.

Kegen closed his eyes, allowing his body to relax in the sensation of having her sleeping by his side. It was just about perfect. Hopefully, she wouldn't freak out when she woke to find him in bed with her.

Chapter Four

Marlowe pried her eyes open taking a look around. Sun filtered in through the window, making the room much brighter than she would have liked at the moment. There wasn't an extra body in her room, but she couldn't say for certain that's how it was last night. She vaguely remembered hearing Kegen talking above her. But was that a memory or fantasy? There was no way she was going to be able to figure that out at the moment. Not without leaving the haven of her bed and definitely not without coffee.

Lifting the sheet Marlowe found she was wearing the bra and panty set she nabbed at Whispers the night before. A little something she picked up last minute before heading over to Tiffany's. At least she remembered that much. Closing her eyes again, she pulled a pillow on top of her head hoping to mute the sun and quiet the commotion in there. She would swear someone was using a sledgehammer, the reverberating pulses were echoing between her ears. Taking a slow calming breath, her senses went into overdrive. A shiver ran down her spine and her mouth watered as arousal swept through her. All she could smell was Kegen's spicy scent. The one that made her want to bury her nose in his chest and just inhale.

She tried to figure out what happened last night. There was the argument with Kegen that lead to him kissing her. The stop at the lingerie boutique then the liquor store, both in hopes of forgetting the argument and the kissing. After that, it was a blur of shots, man bashing, some wine, and margaritas. That's when it got a little fuzzy. She vaguely recalled Steph driving her home but not much else. She was pretty sure she was carried into her house or had learned to levitate.

As she lay there contemplating death and the events of the night, the smell of bacon wafted into the room causing her stomach to roil with nausea. "Is Steph *trying* to make me vomit? God, that woman has a cast-iron stomach." Groggily she scooted to the edge of the bed, waiting with her eyes squeezed shut, praying she wouldn't toss her cookies. After a few breaths, she was finally able to stand up and make her way to the bathroom. Relieving her insistent bladder then washing her hands, she caught a glimpse of the woman in the mirror.

"Ack! Holy shit!" Her hair stuck up in the back, mascara ringed her bloodshot eyes and—she sniffed and scrunched her nose. Grabbing her toothbrush she took care of the worst offense at the moment. Her breath. Alcohol always left a bad taste the morning after and today was no different. Finishing her teeth, she scrubbed her face, and combed out her hair. Popping the cute but not sleep worthy bra off, she grabbed the tank and red flannel shorts she usually slept in off the counter, pulling them on before deeming herself ready to face her friend.

When she walked into the living room, she found the curtains open and a nice warm breeze coming through. "I know I didn't do that."

She turned to say something and was stunned speechless to find Kegen, shirtless, standing in front of her beloved stove. He had on grey sweats pushed low on his hips, showing off the yummiest back dimples she had ever seen in her life. *Dimples of Venus.* Those and six-pack abs made smart women stupid.

Marlowe studied his back dimples for the longest time. She loved licking the warm bronzed skin of those spots. She also loved putting her heels there when she wrapped her legs around him as he fucked her senseless. She and Kegen were the perfect fit.

Kegen turned around, walking to the counter of the island. He was just as gorgeous from the front. Trim waist. Washboard abs. Lightly furred chest. She wanted to run her hands over him, letting her fingers tangle in the hair. It was so soft and springy. She never thought she would like a man with chest hair. Always finding the guys she dated trimmed and waxed. Manscaping could really be overdone at times.

Damn, she loved it when Kegen was standing there all sexy in her kitchen. Usually, he was naked and grabbing some water after a randy bout of sex. She could deal with him partially clothed and cooking if that was his thing. She had no problem sitting on a bar stool ogling him.

At the moment, he held a skillet in one hand as he scooped what looked to be scrambled eggs onto two plates. He hadn't noticed her yet. She was completely torn between gawking at him more and running back to her room, locking the door behind her. With her luck, after last night's small skirmish, he would follow her and give her a lecture on drinking. Maybe she could coax him not to by seducing him.

Before she could decide on a course of action, he set the pan down, wiped his big hands on a dishtowel and looked up, right at her. A slow grin curved one side of his mouth and she was mesmerized. He stopped inches from her, sweeping a lock of her hair behind her ear and running his finger along her jaw. She leaned into the touch and was disappointed when he dropped his hand by his side.

"How you feeling this morning?" His words were low and quiet. Like he assumed her head would be hurting and he didn't want to make it worse. She melted inside a little more. Shit, she really was in love with him. She was doomed.

"I'm fine." Her words came out sounding like she swallowed gravel. She winced and tried to clear her throat, but it didn't do much good.

"Come with me." He took her hand and pulled her along with him to the kitchen. After settling her on one of the bar stools, he walked around the island and poured hot water into her favorite mug before dropping a tea bag in. A teaspoon of honey later, he pushed the cup toward her, waiting patiently for her to drink. "Think you can handle a little food? It's nothing heavy, just some scrambled eggs and bacon. You were out so I ran home and grabbed the stuff."

Marlowe's face flushed. Grocery shopping was on her to-do list for the day. She cleared her throat successfully this time. "Thank you. I might have some eggs. I don't think greasy bacon will agree with me." She smiled shyly and was rewarded with a grin from him. Her heart skipped a beat and she sighed.

She could get used to this kind of treatment. This wasn't the first time he had cooked for her but it was the first breakfast.

He walked around to where she was sitting and gently turned her toward him. He inserted himself between her legs, that serious look she adored on his face. Tension gathered in her belly as his gaze locked onto her lips. Her heart sped up. Arousal screamed through her at his closeness.

"Relax," he whispered. The low timber of his voice sending a shiver down her spine. She nervously licked her lips, unable to do as he said.

Groaning, he mumbled something about needing her, seconds before his lips landed on hers. It was a slow sensual assault of teeth, lips and tongue. Just like he did the night before. He nipped and sipped at her, seducing her into taking part, though that didn't take much. She was all too willing to join in. Her legs came up of their own volition, thighs notching into the dips of his waist as her arms wound around his neck. Butterflies took flight in her stomach as she matched Kegen kiss for kiss. Her heart raced and the longer they explored each other's mouths, the more lightheaded and giddy she felt.

Kegen's hands found their way onto her waist, caressing before snaking around to her ass where he gripped her and pulled her to the edge of the chair. He meshed their lower halves together, his slender hips fitting perfectly into the vee of her thighs. His erection, barely contained behind the soft grey sweats, grew in length and hardened in a matter of seconds. A moan was pulled from her diaphragm as his length pulsed against her core. Marlowe rocked her hips against him, teasing and tormenting herself with what she wanted.

Kegen lifted his head, taking his tempting lips away from hers. "Morning." He placed a quick, soft kiss on her lips then stepped away, moving back into the kitchen.

It didn't escape her notice when he adjusted his erection and winced. A ghost of a smile curved her lips. Always nice to know she had an effect on him.

There was a knock on the door. Before she could hop off the chair and answer it, the door swung open and in walked Rev.

He walked up to her, taking Kegen's place between her thighs and kissed her soundly on the mouth. It was nothing like the kisses she had just gotten from his brother. There was no passion or butterflies accompanying it. She was left confused as to why he would kiss her. He had never done that before.

Rev stepped away like nothing out of the ordinary had happened. "Morning sweetheart." He walked around to the coffee pot and poured himself a cup. "Dish me a plate too. I'm starving."

Marlowe felt a blush take over her body and cast a glance at Kegen. Would he be upset that his brother just kissed her as well? Would he be jealous at all? She wasn't sure. His jaw clenched momentarily before he visibly made himself relax.

"Hey bro, not a good idea." This came from Kegen.

Rev looked at her then back to his brother. "Marking your territory."

"I did that a long time ago."

Rev shrugged and gulped down some coffee. "I don't see the big deal. I do that with Laurel too."

"Yeah and Quin hates it."

Marlowe crossed her arms over her chest, hiding her nipples, which were in hard, tight points thanks to Kegen. He didn't need to know she was turned on.

Pissed off but turned on as well. What was she, a fire hydrant! "Wouldn't it be easier to pee on me?" she deadpanned.

"That's not a kink I want to see." Kegen reached across the island and slid her plate to the middle chair.

She smacked at his hands. "Hey, what the hell are you doing?"

Kegen rounded the counter to stand next to her with his plate and coffee. "Slide over. I don't want to have to look around his ugly mug just to see you."

"What?" She looked to her right; Rev set his plate and coffee down at the place in the middle and started to slide hers back over to where she was sitting. Quickly she moved to the next seat, pushed Rev's things over and pulled her plate in front of her. She didn't want to listen to them bicker because of where they did or didn't sit.

"Hey sweet thing," Rev purred. "I promise I won't bite unless you want me to." He snapped his jaws at her in a playful manner.

Marlowe snorted. "You haven't hit on me in ages. Has your oversexed, male brain snapped? "

Kegen chuckled as he sat down. "How different is a male brain from a female brain?"

"Oh, you'd be surprised."

"I'm sure I would." Kegen winked at her as a grin kicked up one side of his mouth.

She tried to stop it but couldn't, her heart fluttered uncontrollably in her chest, the air was sucked out of her lungs. "Thank you for breakfast."

He beamed a full-blown smile at her this time. It was a damn good thing she was sitting or she would have crumpled to the floor. "Anytime, Peaches."

Marlowe slowly spun her coffee cup. "You aren't mad about last night?"

"Nope." Kegen bit down on a piece of bacon and grinned. It was like she was in some strange twilight zone. Maybe she was still drunk.

Rev snickered next to her so she ignored him.

"Am I still drunk and dreaming?"

"Why would you ask that?"

"You're being so …nice."

"That's because I'm a nice guy. We can talk about last night later. When we don't have a certain audience."

"Oh, I was just hoping we could forget about it and just have sex." She didn't know why that popped out of her mouth. Kegen grinned even bigger and Rev muttered under his breath.

She turned toward him, eyebrow arched in question. "What was that?"

"I said I would. If you wanted to forget a fight and spend the day ravishing my body, I would be all for it."

"I'm sure you would be. I'm still not taking you up on it."

"Don't knock it until you've tried it, sweetheart," Rev said cheekily.

Marlowe laughed and patted his cheek fondly. "I think I'll pass. Kegen is quite enough for me, thanks."

Kegen grabbed her other hand; raising it to his lips, he kissed it. She blushed, realizing what she just admitted to the brothers.

They all turned toward their plates of food and ate. After a couple minutes of silence and between bites of bacon, Rev asked, "How do you feel about him?"

"Him?" Marlowe automatically looked at Kegen.

Rev chuckled. "Yeah, him."

Heat filled her cheeks. Kegen was staring back at her. Arousal and curiosity swam in the dark brown depths of his eyes. "Well," she swallowed hard. "I think that is something he should be asking me, not you."

Rev laughed. "I'm not sure he'll get around to it soon enough for my taste."

Marlowe couldn't help the snort that came out. "Of course, my relationship with Kegen is all about you."

Rev shrugged nonchalantly. "It if wasn't before, then it should be now. I need you two happily committed." Rev got off his chair, grabbing up his dish, and headed to the sink.

Marlowe looked at Kegen, who seemed just as confused as her. "I have no idea what he's talking about. I do want to know how you feel about me, though."

Revlin appeared over Kegen's shoulder. "What are we whispering about?" He grabbed their empty plates breaking the spell around them.

"Nothing that concerns you, little brother," he growled out.

"Oh, I see. Pulling that shit now. Ya know, Marlowe, I *am* younger than him, which means I've got better stamina and a longer life span."

"How does that even make sense, Rev? You were born the same day and I'm guessing within minutes of each other."

"Five minutes to be exact. Still means I'm younger and better looking."

"Oh brother," she groaned.

Rev shrugged and went back to cleaning the rest of the dishes. The man was certifiable.

Kegen draped his arm over her shoulders. "I was hoping for a nice breakfast—just the two of us. Followed up with you and me in the shower." Kegen raked her body with his eyes and she flushed in response. Looking down, she remembered what she was wearing. Her nipples were poking out still, pressing against the soft fabric of the tank top. Her shorts barely covered her, ending at the top of her thighs. "Then spend the rest of the day with you naked and writhing beneath me."

She crossed her arms over her chest, making him chuckle. She scowled. "Are you planning on putting me further under your spell?"

Heat flared in Kegen's eyes. "Hell, yeah. It's one of my favorite positions to have you in."

"You're incorrigible."

He squeezed her shoulder and winked. "I know."

Rev held out the coffee pot. "How about I pour us all a little more then we can move to the living room. Decide what to do today."

Marlowe smiled and nodded. The feeling of family and togetherness rushed over her. She mentally shut the door on the part of her brain that wanted to make more out of what was going on. Let herself just enjoy the moment.

They shuffled out to the living room. Kegen taking a seat on one end of the couch while Rev took the overstuffed chair, leaving her to sit between them. Once she sat down, Kegen pulled her against his side. She curled her legs up and relaxed against him.

"What do you guys want to do today?"

Kegen cleared his throat. "We're having a little get-together at the house today."

"Are you telling me or asking if I want to come?"

"He's asking," Rev replied.

"I don't know. It didn't sound like he was asking." Her eyebrow quirked up in challenge as she looked back to Kegen.

He smirked then asked, "Would you please come over to our house for a casual get-together?"

"Hmmm, I don't know. That wasn't very convincing. What's your definition of casual and do I need to bring anything? As you've seen first hand, I need to go grocery shopping."

"We're going to grill some steaks. Eat too many fattening sides. Listen to a little music while we wait and just hang out. Very casual. Shorts and flip-flops kind of thing. Just bring yourself."

"Since I only need to bring me, then I would be delighted to come Kegen. Thank you." She tilted her head back and kissed him on the cheek. "Out of curiosity, is the *we* in that statement you and Revlin, or are others going to be there? I don't remember you talking about it before."

"Quin and Laurel are coming over. That's all. Mom and Dad are out of town on another RV trip. The rest of the Chute Shack crew went out to Utah to check out a jump site we might be going to next month. If you want to invite Steph over, that's fine by us," Kegen said.

"Yes. Please invite her over so I have someone to flirt with. She doesn't look like she eats much anyway, so we'll have plenty of food," Revlin said.

"Ha! Looks can be deceiving. That woman can eat a wrestler under the table. I've seen it. Won a thousand bucks from it too."

Rev shook his head. "I'll believe that when I see it. I don't know where she would put it all."

"You'll be impressed and quite possibly disgusted. Steph is great. I'll call her and invite her over. I don't know what she has going on today."

"You are the best female friend I've ever had."

"Probably the only one too," Kegen mumbled. He glanced toward the kitchen then looked back at her. Indecision played out on his face. Finally he sighed. "We'll get out of your hair and let you rest up some more or do whatever it is you do after a night out. We need to get home. I need a shower and want to get some work done before kicking back."

Both men stood. Rev pulled her off the couch straight into his arms. He wrapped his arms around her. Leaning down, he whispered in her ear. "He's serious about you. I'm hoping you're just as serious about him. I know you two are meant for each other." He kissed her cheek and passed her to Kegen. "I'll see you a little later, sweetheart."

Kegen gazed down into her face. "What did he say? You look a little pale."

"Nothing for you to worry about. He was just offering up his thoughts on us."

"I'm not sure how I feel about that," he said warily.

Marlowe smiled. "Give me a kiss before I drag you back to my bedroom and tie you to my bed."

"That wouldn't be a bad thing. I really enjoyed it last time."

"I know you did, but Rev is standing at the door waiting for you. I don't think he'll leave without you and I doubt he'll want to do all of the prep work for the barbeque on his own. He couldn't even have breakfast without you cooking for him."

Kegen snorted before he dipped his head, possessing her mouth. He curved his hand around the nape of her neck, tunneling his fingers into her hair. Keeping her in just the right spot in order to feed from her like she was his last meal. She enjoyed every single possessive moment. God, the man could kiss.

Each time he pressed his lips against hers, she felt like she found the other part of her soul.

She shivered and whimpered with growing need. Her arousal soaking her panties, preparing her body for what it hoped would come next. He groaned pulling her tighter against him, pressing them together from thigh to chest. His erection dug into her stomach. Her fingers ached to feel his length in their grasp. To rub over the tip before running up and down his hard shaft.

Reluctantly, and out of a need for oxygen, she tore her mouth from his and gasped for breath. Kegen set her back on her feet and waited until she was steady. His dark eyes glittered with arousal and mutual need.

Right before he turned away, he brushed one more kiss on her lips. "Come over whenever you're ready. I'll be waiting." He walked out the door and in a daze she picked up their forgotten coffee cups and carried them to the kitchen. She glanced at the clock on the microwave and wondered if heading over now would be too soon.

Chapter Five

Kegen glanced at his watch then out the bay window again. "Where the hell could she be?" he muttered unhappily.

Turning from the window, he paced back and forth through the living room a couple more times.

Even though he left her house at ten and it was only now going on three, it felt like an eternity had passed since he was with her last. Not once in his life had a woman had him so tied up in knots that he could barely think, barely breathe.

He actually felt bad now for giving Quin such a hard time when he was chasing after Laurel. Kegen thought his older brother was whipped beyond all recognition when it came to the woman he loved. Now he knew better. Just being apart from Marlowe, knowing she was in her house next door had his nerves jumping.

Unlike Quin, Kegen could march his happy ass over to Marlowe's in a matter of minutes. Fulfill his need to have her in his arms in the time it took Quin to get in his truck to head to Laurel's place. Though that wasn't a problem any more since he moved in with her.

Kegen groaned as memories of what it felt like to be locked between Marlowe's slim thighs this morning teased him. Pressed up against her, he had been in heaven. Even now, he could still feel the heat of her pussy radiating over his dick. The tiny shorts she had on did nothing to dampen how hot and turned on she had been. It took everything in him to not pull her to her bedroom and make love to her, regardless of his brother's presence.

Kegen turned from the window after looking out again and walked back to the kitchen. Grabbing up the steaks, he headed out back to keep busy. The fresh air would do him some good. Hopefully calm him down.

Rev was in the shower and would be out soon.

Quin texted when he and Laurel left and would probably show up in the next ten minutes or so.

Kegen was looking forward to seeing them. Finally introducing them to Marlowe. He couldn't believe in all the time he and Marlowe had been seeing each other, they had never met. The opportunity for it to happen never appeared. Until now.

Kegen was about to put the first steak on the grill when a noise to his right grabbed his attention. He heard the door of the wooden fence open, scraping along the ground, before it was pushed shut. A woman's voice carried to him as she quietly cursed the stubborn door. He smiled imagining Marlowe trying to wrangle the sticky door into place. On the best of days it was a bitch. When it rained—he didn't even bother going through it.

Abandoning the grill, Kegen stealthily walked toward her. With a covered platter in one hand, Marlowe was attempting to shove the door into place with her hip with no success. He grabbed up the plate before it tipped over and shoved the door closed.

Marlowe jumped and squeaked in surprise. Spinning toward him, she whacked him in the chest. "Shit, Kegen! Don't scare me like that."

He grinned and laughed. "Just trying to help, ma'am. How about a kiss for my efforts?"

Marlowe hesitated then rolled her eyes, "I guess." She got up on her tiptoes and placed a light, soft kiss on his cheek. She snatched the plate from his hand and starting walking to the backyard.

"You know, you could have knocked on the front door."

"I did. No one answered so I decided to come in through the gate."

Kegen grunted in response. As she walked in front of him, he found his gaze traveling down to her tight little rear. Clad in khaki shorts, he couldn't take his eyes off it. The shorts were cupping her exquisite ass perfectly. His hands itched to grab hold again. Once was certainly never going to be enough when it came to her. He needed to find something to take his mind off of steering her straight to his bedroom. "How did you know it wasn't Rev coming to your rescue?"

"You don't think I know the difference between you two?"

"I never really thought about it."

"First off, I was able to identify you drunk and near passed out. That's like a super human skill. I talked to Steph and she filled me in on my evening. She said thanks for the invite but she couldn't come. Something came up at home and she had to go handle it. Second, Rev would have snuck up on me and tickled me, not caring what I was doing or holding."

"That's true. Sorry to hear about Steph. Anything we can do to help?"

Marlowe turned and flashed him a winning smile. He was able to drag his eyes away from her ass quick enough she might not have noticed he was staring in the first place. Not that he cared if he was caught staring. She knew he had a thing for her rear. "Nope, but thanks for offering."

Marlowe and Kegen rounded the corner of the house and found Rev at the grill. Her body, already overheated from her brief encounter with Kegen, burst into flames. Rev stood in front of the grill wearing a pair of basketball shorts and nothing else. His hair was still damp from a recent shower and Marlowe couldn't help but watch as a drop of water hit his shoulder and made a beeline heading straight for his chest.

She may not ever want to date the man, but she could damn well drool over him. She would give anything to follow that droplet's path before sucking it into her mouth. It would be even better if it were on Kegen's chest. Without meaning to, a moan slid free.

"Now, Peaches, if I didn't know better, I would say Rev was turning you on."

Kegen's whispered words caressed her ear, sending a riot of goose bumps down her arms. He slipped an arm around her waist and pulled her back into his body. Heat singed every place they touched.

She was turned on all right. She felt breathless and overwhelmed. A visual feast was in front of her; and a smooth, seductive voice and hard body stood behind her. It was a wonder she could string more than two words together. "Reminds me of you," she mumbled.

Kegen's chuckle vibrated through her. Her nipples tightened and shivers ran down her body at the sound.

She needed some space from him or she might just pass out. He was devastating what little self-control she had.

After he and Rev left that morning, she took a long hot shower. She got a little distracted when her thoughts turned to Kegen as she ran a washcloth over her breasts, imagining it was his hands. She skimmed the cloth lower, delving between the lips of her pussy, which were still slick with arousal from Kegen's kisses. She pleasured herself, thinking of Kegen and had been craving the man since.

If they kept traveling down this path, she would be naked and wrapped around Kegen in a heartbeat, not caring who was around. Marlowe dropped her hand down to where he had hold of her and thought about trying to pry free of his grip. She dug her nails in.

"What's going on in that clever brain of yours?"

Turning her head, she had to tilt it back to get a glimpse of his handsome face. A low whimper of need worked its way out of her throat. "I'm wondering if he'll notice you fucking me up against the side of the house. I'm so damn horny, Kegen."

"Me too, Peaches." Kegen smiled devilishly at her, pressing his erection against her backside. She moaned in response. "I promise later we will. I need you as much as you need me." He let go of her waist and stepped around her, taking the heat of his body with him. He snatched the plate from her hands. "Rev, Marlowe brought us a treat. I'm going to go put it in the kitchen."

"Hey beautiful!" Rev called out. When she got next to him, he gave her a quick hug and platonic kiss on the head before going back to his task.

She moved to the end of the grill, turning so she could face the house and slider door. She tried to see where Kegen was inside without letting on that she was looking for him.

"I wondered when you would be over. He's been driving me nuts pacing at that front window all day. I had to take an extra long shower just to get some peace. Marlowe?" He waved his hand in front of her face. "You okay?"

She snapped out of the daze she was in and found Rev looking at her, concern glittering in his eyes. She pasted a friendly smile on her face. "Yeah, I'm good."

Rev looked back at the house just as she did. "What happened?"

"Nothing. I brought cookies. He took them inside." She tried to keep her eyes locked onto his face but was finding it difficult. Rev looked so much like Kegen and his naked flesh wasn't doing a damn thing to douse the arousal swimming in her.

"You think I'm hot, don't you?"

"Don't be an ass." She looked away quickly, but her gaze was drawn back to him. *Where the hell is Kegen?*

Rev took the steaks off the grill, placing them on the waiting plate. He faced her and crossed his arms over his chest. She followed the movement, watching his tattoo flex and bulge just like Kegen's had done the day before.

"Dear god woman, its like you're in a daze. If you look at him with half as much heat as you're looking at me, I'm surprised you're still able to walk. "

Marlowe snorted. "That's just crude, Rev."

"But accurate."

Marlowe wanted to change the subject. Desperately. If they kept on this path, she was going to hunt Kegen down, older brother showing up or not. "Were you trying to start something this morning when you asked me how I felt about him?"

Rev chuckled but didn't answer her question. "You know, this is something that has never happened before."

The slider door opened and out walked a stunning brunette. Her hair was pulled back into a ponytail that made her eyes and cheekbones stand out. She was slim and casually dressed in a light pink tank top, Capri jeans and sparkly sandals that showed off her pink tipped toenails. "What's never happened before?"

Revlin grinned and walked over to the woman. He wrapped her up in a bear hug, lifting her off her feet. "Laurel! I knew one day you'd want a real man. Have you finally seen the light and tossed my older brother aside?"

Laurel giggled and pushed out of Rev's arms. A man who Marlowe could only guess was Quin, because he looked so much like the twins, walked up behind Laurel, wrapped his arms around her, and pulled her back into his body. "No," he said flatly. "As a matter of fact," he lifted Laurel's left hand and stuck it out for all to see. "She's agreed to marry me."

"No shit! It's about damn time," Rev said grabbing Laurel's hand examining the rock on her finger. "Damn, sweetheart, he must really like you."

Laurel laughed and pulled her hand from his. "You're such a dork Revlin Ferris. Don't ever change."

Marlowe was beginning to think she should leave when Kegen walked out of the house. His gaze locked with hers and he smiled. Nothing big or dazzling. Just a friendly, curved up on one side, sexy tilt to his lips that froze the breath in her lungs, kind of smile.

"Congratulations you two," Kegen said, hugging them both briefly before coming to her side, which brought their attention to her.

"Oh," Laurel exclaimed. "I didn't know you had company." She smiled brightly at Marlowe and Marlowe couldn't help but smile back. The woman exuded warmth and friendliness.

Kegen wrapped his arm around her shoulders, tucking her against him before introducing her. "This is my girlfriend, Marlowe."

"Oh, the infamous girlfriend. I'm Laurel and this is my fiancé Quin." With a dazzling smile, Laurel indicated the man hovering over her shoulder. "We were beginning to wonder if Kegen made you up."

The women laughed. Marlowe had wondered the same thing about them at times. "It's very nice to meet you both and congratulations on the engagement."

Laurel's gazed bounced between Marlowe and Kegen. "So, you're their neighbor?"

"Yes, I live right next door, over there." She pointed to her house off to her left.

"Which one tried seducing you first?" Laurel mock whispered.

"Laurel," Quin warned. "We talked about this."

Laurel harrumphed. "Fine. Bland, boring topics it is." Her fingers drummed against Quin's arm, which was still wrapped around her. The corner of her mouth lifted and Marlowe saw a mischievous gleam enter her eyes. "Do you wear the lingerie from your store for him?"

"Honey, you promised," Quin groaned.

Rev and Kegen laughed at Quin's obvious discomfort. Marlowe smirked and shot a glance at Kegen. "I wear it all of the time. I'm hoping to get this new line of men's wear in and have him give me a private show. Mesh boxers. Tiny boxer shorts that leave nothing to the imagination. Itty bitty man-thongs."

Laurel cackled in delight.

Kegen leaned down to whisper in her ear. "You know I like going commando. Easier to get my dick out quick when you drive me crazy with lust."

Marlowe's eyes opened wide. Kegen said it loud enough for them to all to hear.

"Alright then," Quin said into the silence. "Any chance I can get the family discount now?"

Marlowe couldn't contain the shock she knew was washing over her face. "We aren't family."

Quin snorted, "Not yet." He high-fived Kegen before turning away. "Come on, let's eat, I'm starving." Quin scooped up Laurel, tossing her over his shoulder. She squealed and smacked him on the butt.

"You're always starving," Laurel complained light-heartedly. "But we came here for food."

"Bro, not in front of the young and impressionable." Rev grabbed the plate with the steaks on it and followed the couple inside, leaving Kegen and Marlowe alone.

Her entire body stiffened under Kegen's arm. "I think we need to talk," Marlowe said, as a new kind of fear tried to clog her throat. Kegen didn't seem the least bit put off by his brother's words.

Kegen kissed the top of her head. "I agree."

Marlowe broke away from Kegen to stand in front of him. She wanted to see his face full on and try to figure out what he was thinking. "We'll do it soon?" There were things she needed to know. Things he needed to know.

He grinned, raising his hand holding up three fingers. "I promise."

Marlowe rolled her eyes. She couldn't even stay worried about what was going on. A sexy as hell smile was curving Kegen's beautiful lips. Mischief twinkled in his dark eyes. His unruly black hair fell forward, practically begging her to run her fingers through it.

"Were you even a Boy Scout?"

"Only one way to find out." Kegen leaned in close and all too briefly she got to experience the feel of his lips against hers.

As he moved away, she curled her fingers into his shirt to steady herself. "I'm going with no," she murmured.

Kegen only grinned and held his hand out for her to take. She looked at it, then back to his face. She knew then that by placing her hand in his larger one, she would find her future. Was she ready for that?

Chapter Six

Kegen held his breath waiting for Marlowe to take his hand. He could see the emotions crossing her face. Worry. Indecision. Fear. Hope.

He sensed he was missing something important. Something that was crucial to their relationship. But never in his life had he wanted something as bad as this. He didn't know why but the moment felt significant.

Minutes ticked by as tension filled the air around them.

Marlowe took a huge breath and let it out.

A wave of relief rushed through him when she slid her trembling hand into his. His heart tumbled and he took a shaky breath. They still had a lot to discover about each other. This would be the start. This was when he would say their relationship really started.

Together, they silently walked inside the house.

Quin, Laurel and Rev were all sitting at the table talking. The second they entered the room, the group went quiet and all eyes fell on them. Laurel grinned and broke the uncomfortable tension beginning to rise. "We wondered if you two got lost. I apologize for Quin's comment. He tends to get ahead of himself at times. Thinks he knows everything. *All* of them do actually."

"Really?" Marlowe questioned, a glint of humor in her eyes. "I never had that problem with Rev."

Laurel leaned forward, eyes brimming with excitement. "Oh? You know, I've heard they generally like the same women. Is that..." Kegen abruptly cut her off.

"You can stop right there, Laurel. Marlowe never dated Rev," he announced in a no-nonsense voice.

"Not that I didn't try," Rev said.

Kegen steered Marlowe to the end of the table away from his twin and next to Quin. He wasn't sure his older brother was the safest option, but it would have to do. Kegen held out her chair and waited for Marlowe to sit before he took his own seat. She leaned around him to look at Rev. "You didn't try to date me. You only flirted like a two-bit whore."

Kegen choked on the swallow of beer he had just taken as everyone else laughed.

"That's exactly how he acted with Laurel," Quin said. "He couldn't keep his hands off her. I told him she was mine. He refused to listen. You're going to have to try a different tactic little brother if you plan on finding a wife."

"Good thing I'm not in the market for one. I have no desire to change my social status like you and Kegen." Rev grinned like an idiot and they all shook their heads.

"He's gonna fall so hard," Laurel said evilly. "I can't wait."

Kegen glanced around the table as everyone went back to eating. He smiled at the sight around him. His older brother was happier than he'd ever seen. Rev was texting in between bites of food and seemed pretty satisfied with his life. Kegen figured that was good for now. Rev was right when he said love would find a way whether you were ready or not. Kegen figured it would hit Rev out of the blue, much like a Mack truck.

Kegen slipped his hand onto Marlowe's knee and squeezed. She turned her head toward him and smiled contentedly before going back to the conversation she was having. He wasn't surprised when she laid her hand on top of his under the table. That came when she slid her hand further up, gliding it over his erection. Arousal steamrolled through him at her touch. Laurel was looking at him with a knowing smile on her face. Grinning back, he winked and joined their conversation pulling Rev in with him.

Laurel and Marlowe refused to let the guys do the dishes. They forced them outside to start the fire pit and to give them some time to catch up. It was the perfect time for Marlowe to ask her new friend a few questions and get another woman's take on the guys. Specifically Kegen.

Laurel stood in front of the sink rinsing the dishes off before handing them to Marlowe to put in the dishwasher.

"So, how long have you and Quin been together?" Marlowe asked. She knew they had recently reconnected and that they were pretty serious according to Rev, but she didn't know they were to the let's-get-married stage.

"About seven months. We knew, well *I* knew Quin in high school. He was the hottest, most popular boy in school. He had no idea who I was, of course. I was a little geeky and a lot shy back then. Our paths crossed once and all I'll say is that it wasn't a great experience for me. We ran into each other again, thanks to my cousin, when I was assigned a skydiving look book. We've been together ever since."

"Wow, and now you're getting married? That's—wow."

Laurel laughed lightly. "Yeah, Quin said I was lucky to get the time I did. If it had been up to him, we would have been married months ago. It was pressing it letting him move in with me after a month of dating. I don't think I would have handled him popping the question at the same time very well."

"So when a Ferris boy finds someone he wants, he really goes for it, doesn't he?" Marlowe leaned back against the counter.

Laurel turned the water off and faced her. "Yes, he does. I take it Kegen is pretty serious."

"I don't know. Rev says he is. From his reaction tonight about Quin's comment, I would guess he is. He just hasn't told me."

"That's a Ferris for you. They assume you know exactly what they're thinking."

"Great. I failed my mind-reading class."

"I know what you mean. I have no idea what's going on in Quin's mind most of the time. The first time I came over here, it was after one of the jumps. Quin was all over me when we were out at the Chute Shack. Holding my hand. Kissing me. Generally being this super attentive guy. So I'm thinking he's into me. I get here and he barely talks to me while Rev *and* Kegen flirt the entire time. They only did it to mess with him. I knew that. But Quin acts like someone stole his favorite toy and storms out of the house like a child. Perplexing, I tell ya. It was enough to send me packing."

Marlowe's head bobbed in agreement. "That's like yesterday. I was waiting for my friend and I'm watching the guys unload one of the trucks. Kegen takes his shirt off and runs it down his chest, then he does this head nod come-hither thing and I shake my head no. I knew he was going back to work and I had plans. He gestures for me to come over again and I, again, say no. Then I see him mumble like he's annoyed with me and gets all pissy. If he really wanted to see me then he should have come over and talked to me."

"This shirt thing? I think I need to hear more about that."

"Lusting after your future brother-in-law?" Marlowe giggled when Laurel groaned.

"No. It just sounds…intriguing. The guys are hot."

"Yeah, they are," Marlowe drawled.

Tuning to the window that looked out back, Marlowe fixed her gaze on Kegen. He sat with his brothers drinking a beer. He was relaxed, kicked back in a lounger, laughing at something Quin said. His eyes danced with amusement. The tense lines around his mouth were gone. He looked happy and Marlowe found she loved that look on him. She wanted to head out there and sit next to him. Bask in the contentment radiating off him.

"They do look so much alike. If I didn't know better, I would think they were triplets."

"Yeah, they call themselves Irish Triplets, bastardizing the Irish Twins definition. I can't imagine having three boys all born the same year. It would have driven me nuts. I'm sure that's why their parents are always off in the RV somewhere. They finally don't have to worry *as much* as they used to about them. Not now that the business is doing well and at least one of them is settling down."

"How did you and Quin manage to find your happily ever after? It doesn't sound like things were going well in the beginning."

"He got over his fit when he found out I was meeting up with an old friend who happened to be a guy. By the time he found me, I was drunk as a skunk. He took care of me and after that, I don't know, he just was always there calling and texting. He made his mind up that he wanted to be part of my life and there he was *and* still is."

"Well, Kegen saw me drunk last night, or more accurately, this morning. My friend got him to help her. I'm just glad I didn't throw up on him."

"Did he stay the night?" Laurel asked lightly.

Not one to really tell tales, Marlowe found she didn't mind sharing the details with Laurel. It must have been the sense of camaraderie she felt with the woman. Each of them with a Ferris in their life. "Yeah, but I was oblivious to it though. I was surprised to see him standing in my kitchen cooking breakfast this morning"

Laurel laughed and came up next to Marlowe. "Now that's a sight I wouldn't mind waking up to. But with Quin doing the cooking and only wearing an apron. He's got the cutest ass I've ever seen." She sighed dreamily. "Their momma definitely raised those boys right."

Kegen took that exact moment to catch Marlowe's eye. He shot her a look that made her pulse race and her body tingle. Lust and desire gleamed back at her. There was a cocky half grin gracing his lips and, to top it off, he winked.

"It looks like Kegen is definitely into you. I hope it works out Marlowe. They're really great guys once you get to know them."

Marlowe and Laurel moved away from the window as all three men got up from the loungers. "You know you should come to the Chute Shack with us next weekend. They guys are practicing for some upcoming competition. I'd love the company."

"You don't jump?"

"No. Small, cramped spaces are not my thing. Quin got me on the plane while it was on the ground once." Laurel shuddered. "I started to hyperventilate and almost passed out. He said he never wanted to see me go through that again."

Quin walked through the slider door. "I've never seen anything scarier."

Laurel crinkled her nose and stuck out her tongue.

Quin walked up to her and wrapped his arms around her. "Are you two coming outside or are you going to spend your evening staring out the window at us? You've got towels to wipe up the drool, right?"

"You wish," she murmured seconds before Quin growled and dropped a kiss on her lips.

Rev came in next, not batting an eye at Laurel and Quin's lip lock. "If you're trying to figure out who's better looking, I'll save you the trouble—I am." His phone beeped and he paused as he checked it out. He stifled a laugh and kept walking further into the house.

Kegen was the last to walk in. He didn't stop next to her and she was sadly disappointed. Instead, he went to the pantry. "You guys want S'mores? We have the stuff for them."

Marlowe clapped her hands gleefully, dispelling her disappointment. "Yes! I love those. Especially the burning of the marshmallow."

Kegen snorted. "You know you aren't supposed to actually let them catch fire and burn, right?"

"Uh, how else would I get burnt marshmallow?"

Kegen chuckled. "Come help me with this stuff."

Marlowe went over to him and casually bumped him with her hip. "Having a good time with your brothers?"

"Yeah. Thanks for giving us some time to talk. Seems the only time we see Quin is at work and, well, we have to work. Not much time to shoot the shit."

"I figured as much. I know you're close to your brothers."

"We're a close-knit kind of family," he agreed nodding his head.

Marlowe smiled stiffly. "That's nice."

Kegen sighed, hooked her by the belt loops, and leaned back against the wall pulling her with him. Her hands landing on his chest so she didn't smash him in the face. "You know, I don't think I've ever heard you talk about your family."

Marlowe worked to keep her face neutral. "Nothing to say about them really."

"I'm sure that's not true."

Marlowe shrugged. She always felt uncomfortable talking about her parents. That was one of the reasons she kept her heart from getting attached. Steph was the only one fully entrenched in her background.

"Come on, Marlowe, give me something. It can't be that bad."

"My Mom is dead and my Dad lives a couple of hours from here. We don't talk so…" She broke off, letting the words hang out there.

"Jesus Peaches, I'm sorry."

"It isn't a big deal. Mom died years ago when I was a teen. Dad…we just don't get along well. He stays out of my life, I stay out of his."

Kegen's narrowed, analytical gaze and tightly clenched jaw made her wish she hadn't told him. "I'm fine you know. I don't need to talk about it or have you feel sorry for me. I got over everything years ago. Just ask Steph."

Wrapping a hand around the nape of her neck, he pulled her toward him. Kissing her soundly on the lips, he leaned back. "I will."

Pushing off his chest, it didn't take much to break his hold on her waist. Turning back to the pantry, she grabbed graham crackers, chocolate bars and the bag of marshmallows. As she was making her way outside, she ran into Rev.

"You okay?" he whispered.

No, but she wasn't telling him that. "Yeah." Together they walked outside to the fire pit. Quin and Laurel joined them a couple of minutes later. Five minutes after that, Kegen walked out. A look of determination etched onto his face. He wasn't going to let what she said about her parents go quite as easily as most did.

Chapter Seven

"You guys drive home safe," Kegen called out to Quin and Laurel right before he shut the front door. It was after midnight by the time they all decided to call it a night. Rev was crashed in front of the TV along with Marlowe, who looked to be asleep.

He was ready to crash. They both had to work tomorrow, well later, and while he didn't need to go in until around noon, he didn't think it was the same for her.

As much as he wanted to drag her back to his bed, but not knowing her schedule, he figured it would be best to take her home.

Before he woke her though, it wouldn't hurt to change into something a bit more sleep worthy. With any luck, he could crawl into bed with her and wrap his body around hers.

Kegen took off down the hall, brushed his teeth and changed. He was back out in the living room in less than five minutes.

Walking over to the couch, he sat down next to her. He took her hand in his, caressing the soft skin with his thumb. "Hey, Peaches," he whispered. "You ready to go home?"

She grunted and gradually opened her eyes. "You mean we aren't already?"

"Sorry, honey. We're still at my place."

She woke up a little more. "You're coming with me, right?"

Damn, he loved that sleep-filled voice of hers. He nodded his head eagerly.

Stretching her arms over her head, Marlowe thrust her breasts out and he couldn't help but notice. She dropped her arms and sat up. Her gaze landed on Rev. "He gonna be okay there?"

"Yeah, he'll be good. Wouldn't be the first time he fell asleep out here."

Leaning over, she kissed him before patting his leg. "Let's go then." She glanced at Rev again, worry written across her face. "Maybe you should leave him a note or something so he doesn't come looking for us."

"I won't," Rev mumbled. He opened his eyes, looking at them from beneath his lashes.

Marlowe crawled across the couch until she was next to his brother. Wrapping her arms around him she hugged him tight. "Thanks for having me over. I had a nice time." She pecked him on the cheek before scrambling off the couch.

Rev got off the couch and walked past them. "Night lovebirds. Good thing we go in late, bro. I hope you have someone opening up Whispers for you, Marlowe. Otherwise, you're going to be hurting."

"Thanks for your concern, Rev. Monica has the early shift. You remember her, right? Dark hair. Nice ass. Great rack. If I recall, you tried luring her into one of the dressing rooms so you could seduce her and she shot you down."

Rev perked right up. "Monica? Yeah, I remember her. Maybe I'll pop in and see how she's doing. Try my luck again."

Marlowe snickered. "You're going to need more than good luck."

"Night, Rev."

"Night." He followed them to the door and locked it after they left. The loud snick of the lock a clear sign that he didn't expect to see Kegen again until much later.

"Key," Kegen asked as they stepped up on Marlowe's porch.

Marlowe reached out and turned the knob on the door, swinging it open.

Kegen frowned. "You didn't lock the door?"

"No. I never do when I'm at your house. I never saw the need when I was so close."

"In general, I would agree, but don't do it again. You never know who will be in the area and decide they want to get into a pretty girl's house."

"They would have to know a pretty girl lived there first, Kegen."

"Still, please don't do that again. Maybe I should take a look around. Make sure no one else is here." He made a furtive glance in the direction of her bedroom.

"I'm sure its fine, Kegen. I would think if anyone was in here and they wanted to get me, they would have made themselves known by now. Let's go to bed. I'm exhausted and I want to snuggle you." She grabbed his hand and led him back to the bedroom. After turning down the sheets, she went to the bathroom, brushed her teeth, went pee and put on her jammies. Nothing fancy this time. He looked just as tired as she was.

When she walked back out into the bedroom, she found Kegen propped up in the middle of her bed. One of the nightstand lamps was turned on; casting a glow across his chest was bare. She could just make out the desire in his smoldering eyes. If he thought she was going to just climb in bed and fall asleep without any of his loving, then he was wrong.

Marlowe came to the side of the bed. She fidgeted momentarily, not knowing what to do.

Kegen's head tilted, "You okay?"

She let her eyes roam over his exposed body. "More than okay." She licked her lips before stripping out of her clothes and climbing onto the bed. Perched at the edge, she slowly crawled toward him, imagining all of the things he wanted to do to him. Her eyes darted to the straps still attached to the slats of the headboard.

"Not tonight, Peaches."

She exaggerated her pout, even though she really wasn't upset. Halfway across the bed, she realized she should grab a condom. Scooting backward, Kegen's eyes widened and he opened his mouth, no doubt to protest.

"We need a condom."

He snorted and nodded. The feral smile back on his face.

Once she got what she needed, she didn't waste time crawling seductively across the bed again. She tossed him the protection, and while he was busy catching it, she darted across, straddling his comforter-covered legs.

"You might want to pull the sheets down," he said, his voice low and aroused.

"In good time. I want to tease a bit first."

"Isn't that what we've been doing all day? Teasing each other with what we couldn't have at the time? Trust me, I'm more than ready for you." He put his hand on the comforter at his waist and pushed it and the sheets down low enough for his cock to spring free.

Marlowe leaned forward and without preamble, swallowed him whole. Kegen groaned. His body lifted off the bed. Hands fisted the fabric still in his hands. "Fucking hell."

Marlowe used her tongue and lips to work him over. Loving the salty tang of Kegen's pre-cum. Intending only use her mouth to drive him beyond reason, she hollowed her cheeks on the way up his length before driving down until her lips reached the base of his cock. He jolted and convulsed above her.

"Enough," he growled. He easily flipped her on her back before coming over her. The predatory gleam in his eyes causing her pussy to ripple in anticipation.

He ripped the condom open and sheathed himself, in the space of a heartbeat. At least one of them was still thinking straight.

Scooping her legs up, he draped them over his arms then used them to pulled her toward him until the head of this thick cock nudged her opening.

"Do it," she whispered harshly. "You know I love it when you get rough."

Kegen dug the fingers of one hand into her thigh, holding her in place with his steely grasp. Bending over her, he planted his other hand next to her head so he could whisper in her ear. "Not tonight, Peaches."

Sinking his hard cock in inch by inch, he pushed deep through the sensitive tissue of her pussy until he could go no further. She quaked beneath him at the exquisite ecstasy of finally having him in her.

"All night, Marlowe. I want to stay buried in you all night, but I want you too damn much right now."

Kegen pulled back ever so slowly before plunging in again. Over and over he repeated the process. The slow withdraw while she clenched her inner muscles in an attempt to keep him inside, then a harsh, forceful thrust forward. She gasped and bowed under him. The spark of her orgasm built into an intense flame. She wouldn't be able to stand much more.

Kegen leaned back, jerking her legs higher, lifting her ass off the bed as he jack hammered into her. The slick, wet sounds of their bodies washed over her ears.

"Do it," he demanded, his voice rough and strained.

She knew what he was talking about. She slid her hand over her belly making a beeline for her clit. It wouldn't take much to set her off.

"Now, Peaches," he cried out harshly.

She pressed her finger to her clit and all it took was a brush or two against it. She cried out his name as she fell over the edge. Her pussy clenched and held him captive. Milking him into following right behind her.

Kegen collapsed on top of her. Struggling to catch his breath. All too soon he rolled away. She was pleased to see his legs weren't steady as he edged off the bed and went to the bathroom. He came out a few seconds later with a warm washcloth, cleaned her up and disappeared into the bathroom again.

Marlowe thought about looking for her pajamas but didn't have the energy required. Crawling over the bed, she slipped under the covers and waited for him to come back.

Kegen climbed in next to her, pulling her against his warm body.

"Now that's how an evening should end." She yawned the last part.

He pressed a kiss to the top of her head. "I agree. Night, Marlowe."

She brushed her lips against his skin. "Night, Kegen." She drifted to sleep knowing she was safe and protected in Kegen's arms.

Chapter Eight

Monday morning came screaming in with a rush. Marlowe's alarm clock was blaring a wild tune, someone was pounding on the front door and Kegen wasn't in bed like he should have been.

Oh, she remembered bringing him to bed last night and, as far as she was concerned, he should still be there.

The door to the bathroom opened and he walked out, sadly with his shirt on. Pausing next to the bed, he turned the alarm off before leaning down to kiss her. "Morning."

"Morning," she sighed as he stepped away.

"Sounds like someone really needs you at the door. I'll get it while you roll that cute ass of yours out of bed." She watched, mesmerized by the fit of his sweats, as he went out the door shutting it behind him.

She flopped back wishing this wasn't the way they were starting their morning. Two more seconds of her private pity party and she was ready to get up and face the day. Hopefully, it wasn't one of the girls from the boutique coming by with a problem.

Getting out of bed, she dashed into the bathroom. A quick shower, a couple minutes in front of the mirror and a pit stop for clothes, and she was as put together as she was going to get at the moment.

Pulling the door open, she heard voices coming from the kitchen. Kegen and Rev were standing around the coffee pot. They both looked in her direction as she came out.

"Morning Rev, you're over here awfully early."

"Yeah, came to get Kegen."

Marlowe joined the guys in the kitchen. Kegen handed her a coffee then snagged her around the waist, pulling her against him. The warmth of his body enveloped her and she sighed. "I thought you didn't have to go in until later. It's only nine, right?"

"Yep, sure is, but our bossy older brother called with a change of plans. A group of clients needed to move up their timetable."

"Ah, and the client always comes first."

"You know it, doll." Rev tipped back his mug and swallowed down the rest of his drink. "Go say your goodbyes, bro. We need to be out the door in twenty."

Rev kissed her on the cheek then left.

"There goes my plan to make you breakfast again," Kegen said ruefully.

Marlowe patted his arm before moving out of the shelter of his arms. She puttered around the kitchen as they talked. "Maybe another day. Since we don't get to spend the morning together, I'll probably go into work. There's always stuff to be done."

Kegen drained his cup then put it in the sink alongside his brother's. "Okay. How about dinner tonight? Just you and me."

Passing by in front of Kegen again, he reached out and grabbed her wrist, drawing her into him. He wrapped his arms around her loosely. "How about it?"

She looked up into his handsome face and melted at the eager look there. "Yeah. I'd like that."

He dropped a gentle kiss on her lips. "Good. Meet back here around six?"

Marlowe thought over what she had planned for the day. Lingerie to order. Research into adding that new line for men. Start working on the catalog. Not too much in the grand scheme of things. Since she was going in early, it would be no problem taking off when she wanted. "I can manage that. I'll hit the store and get stuff for pasta."

"Great. I need to go. Quin will kick my ass if we're late." He cupped her face, stared at her with beautiful brown eyes, and then lowered his head. His lips whispered across hers, warm and gentle. He pulled away before she could press into him further. She wanted more but knew they were running out of time. "I'll see you tonight."

Marlowe walked Kegen to the door, watched his fine ass walk home, and took a much-needed breath before switching over to work mode. She loved running the lingerie boutique. Finding pretty, lacy, silky, see-through things. Helping women of all shapes and sizes find the perfect item to make them feel beautiful and feminine. Having a huge selection of seductive undergarments at her fingertips for when she had a date.

Racing through the house, she gathered up her purse and briefcase, poured coffee in her to-go mug and was out the door within ten minutes of Kegen leaving. The quicker she got to work, the quicker she could pick flirty but not too over-the-top undergarments and get her work done for the day. A stop at the war bar next door to her shop would be necessary too.

Marlowe stood in the middle of her living room at a loss as to what to do. She looked at the clock in the kitchen again. The agreed upon meeting time of six o'clock had passed an hour and a half ago and she still hadn't heard from Kegen. Not one word via text or phone. She tried calling him but it went straight to voicemail.

Worrying her bottom lip, she hoped nothing had happened to him. Lord knew the many different things that could go wrong when jumping from an airplane with only a thin silk parachute between you and certain death.

She glanced at the dining room table. The candles were burning down quicker than she hoped. The wine had so much time to breathe it probably wasn't good anymore and the food was horribly cold. Maybe it wasn't the best idea to dish out the food before he got there. She just assumed he would be on time.

The rumble of a truck pulled her out of her frantic thoughts. Rushing to the front door, she grabbed the handle then hesitated. Did she rush out there and demand to know what was going on? Yell at him for not being on time and not calling to let her know he was going to be late? Or did she wait for him to come to her?

Oh god, it shouldn't be this difficult. Still, she never opened her door. She did peek out the small window next to it though. Kegen was walking around the back of the truck, mouth in a sever frown, heading for the passenger side. Pulling the door open he held his hand out and waited. Rev stuck his head out the door, said something she couldn't figure out then twisted in his seat and hopped down on one foot. It took her a second to realize why. He was injured. His left foot was encased in a medical boot.

Marlowe was out the door in a flash, running across their lawns. She skidded to a halt next to Kegen. "Holy shit, what happened?"

"Hey, doll," Rev said all smiles.

"Don't you hey doll me like everything is hunky-dory. What did you do? Are you okay? Do you need anything?" She stepped up to him to visually inspect him. He didn't look too worse for wear. No scratches or bruises. The black Chute Shack shirt he was wearing was in prefect shape as were his shorts.

"I'm good. Just had a little accident at work. Messed up my ankle." He stuck the injured limb in front of him.

"I can see that." As relief poured through her, irritation started to build. She spun on Kegen. "Why didn't you call me and let me know?"

"There wasn't anything you could have done while I waited around. You would have been bored out of your mind." He said it all so calmly, like she hadn't been worrying about him for the last hour and a half.

"But what about," that was all she got out before Rev hopped toward her.

"As much as I can't wait to listen to Marlowe ream you, bro, I'd much rather do it inside while prone on the couch. I'm starving, tired and my damn leg is starting to bother me."

Kegen looked confused at his brother's statement. Apparently, he didn't think he had done anything to warrant a reaming. He glanced at her before moving to his brother's side. "Can you shut the truck door for me, Marlowe?"

"Sure." Slamming it shut, she watched as the twins shuffled to the house. She didn't know whether to follow them or not. Surely they wouldn't want her hovering, given how he didn't want her to wait with him at the hospital, which she would have gladly done.

This was exactly why she didn't let herself get too involved. She was worked up into an emotional frenzy and the guy didn't think she was important enough to call.

Walking back to her house, as soon as she went through the door and her eyes fell on the dining room table, she had an idea. No reason for all of the food to go to waste. He may not have needed her earlier, but maybe she could help out now.

"You're going to make a fool out of yourself," she mumbled. Sighing with self-disgust.

That didn't stop her though. As quick as she could, she scooped everything into containers, and then all of it went into a bag. She made plenty of mushroom ravioli, breadsticks, and salad for the three of them. Granted, she planned on having the leftovers for lunch the next day, but she would survive without it.

She blew out the candles, popped a stopper back in the wine before putting it in the bag with the food and was out the door in no time. A change in her plans for the evening but, hopefully, the guys, or at least Rev, would appreciate it. She didn't know where she stood with Kegen at the moment.

Knocking on the guys' door, she didn't bother to wait for anyone to answer. Rev was sprawled out on the couch; head tilted back, eyes closed while Kegen was in the kitchen yelling out what they had in the fridge.

"How about we just have the dinner I made," she asked as she walked in.

Rev's head popped up. "You are an angel. Kegen, she brought food. Must be the dinner she made for your date tonight."

Kegen walked out of the kitchen and toward her, shoulders slumped. "Damn. I forgot."

Instead of letting it show how much that statement hurt, Marlowe pasted on a smile and handed the bag to him. "You're going to want to heat it back up. I'll be in to help in a couple of minutes. I want to check on your brother."

Kegen nodded stiffly before heading back to the kitchen. His eyes betraying nothing of what he was thinking.

Marlowe sat on the coffee table in front of Rev. "Are you really okay?"

"Yeah. Only thing hurt is my ankle and my pride."

"How'd it happen?"

Rev grimaced as a blush heated his cheeks. "It was the stupidest thing. You don't want to hear about it."

"I definitely do now."

He scrubbed his hands over his face and mumbled. "I wasn't paying attention and tripped over some rigging in the hanger. It was a complete fluke that I actually sprained my ankle this bad."

"I'm so sorry." Marlowe could see that it was bothering him but, at the same time, she had a pretty good idea why he tripped. She couldn't stop the giggle that got out. He glared at her, which only made her giggle more. "There was a woman involved in this *not paying attention* wasn't there?"

He groaned and bounced his head off the back of the couch. "Yes."

Marlowe dropped her head down and pressed her lips together to suppress the laugh that wanted out. She cleared her throat a couple of times and when she looked back up, Rev was staring at her. "It's not funny," he said drolly.

"Actually, it is. You were trying to impress her, weren't you?"

"Yes, he was. One of the clients. Tall, skinny, bleached blonde woman. Had her nose turned up at him the entire day then they were put together for the tandem. He must have done some smooth talking while they were on the plane. By the time they landed, she was a giggling mess of besotted woman." Kegen strode out of the kitchen carrying a plate of food.

Marlowe jumped up. "I was going to come and help."

He handed her the plate without a word, went to the end of the couch, then shoved his arms under Rev's armpits and yanked him up. He grabbed the plate from her and shoved it at Rev. "Your dinner is served."

Taking her hand, Kegen pulled her into the kitchen. Once they were alone, he wrapped his arms around her and squeezed. "I'm so sorry, Marlowe. Everything got away from me when Rev got hurt."

Marlowe wrapped her arms around Kegen and held on. Breathing deeply, she waited until that sense of calm enveloped her. "I understand. I was worried you were the one that got hurt. Remind me to never look up skydiving accidents again. It might be better if I don't know what can happen."

Kegen leaned back. "Damn, honey, I'm sorry. Skydiving is a high-risk sport but we have so many safety measures in place. Not to mention, we own and maintain our own planes. Keep up on the latest technology and designs for harnesses and gear. We go through refresher training and do our best to supply the safest atmosphere possible. We take every precaution to be as safe as possible. We just didn't factor in when someone tries to impress a pretty lady and trips over his own forgotten equipment."

"I heard that," Rev yelled form the living room.

Marlowe and Kegen laughed. Getting up on tiptoes, she kissed him quick and hard. "I'm hungry, you ready to eat?"

"More than you know." The sexual tension between them rose. She held her breath waiting to see what would happen next. When he led her to the table where he had their food and wine, a thread of disappointment wound through her.

They ate in silence for a while, until Rev decided he didn't like being alone.

"Marlowe, I can't reach the remote. Do you mind coming in here and getting it for me?" Rev whined.

"You know you're not allowed to watch TV while you eat, Rev. Mom said so."

"Mom would let me. I'm hurt." She could hear the pout in his voice.

"How about I call her, tell her what happened and see what she says?" Kegen rolled his eyes and shook his head. Quietly to her he said, "She's going to throw a fit when she finds out how he got hurt. He may be the baby, but acting foolish and getting injured stopped getting him sympathy from her when we moved out. At least that's what she claims. We haven't had anything happen to test what she said. We'll see how she really reacts if I get desperate enough to call her."

Rev didn't say anything for a couple of minutes. They heard the clang of his plate on the coffee table followed by a sad sigh. "It sure is lonely out here. I wish someone would eat dinner with me. I'm thirsty too. I didn't get a drink."

Marlowe and Kegen shared a look. "Not going to have the kind of evening I was hoping," Kegen said.

"Doesn't look like it. It was nice to have dinner with you though."

"It was delicious too, thank you."

She got up from her chair, "No problem." Picking up their plates, she went to the sink and washed them off, sticking them in the dishwasher. She leaned against the sink once she was done. "I have to get going. I cut out a little early to get dinner ready. There's some work I need to get done before heading in tomorrow."

Kegen moved in front of her, placing his hands firmly on her waist. "I really am sorry about forgetting."

His phone buzzed in his pocket. While he was distracted by it, she took the time to study him. His black hair swung forward, brushing against his cheeks. She wanted to reach up and move it out of the way so she could see more of his face. Try to read what was going on in his mind. There really was no reason why she shouldn't, once she thought about it. So she did. The soft wisps of his hair glided through her fingers, electrifying her skin. Gripping it in her hands fascinated her, as he went down on her.

Heat bloomed across her cheeks when Kegen stopped what he was doing and looked at her. The grin on his face telling her he knew what she was thinking. "I should probably give you Quin and Laurel's numbers just in case. That way you can text them if you can't get hold of me. I don't want you to worry unnecessarily."

She licked her suddenly dry lips. "Thanks. So, I guess I'll get going. Lots of work to do before I turn in."

Kegen's gaze dropped to her lips quickly before meeting hers again. "Yeah," he grunted. "I need to help knucklehead out there get ready for bed."

"Okay." Looping her hands around his neck, she pulled him down until their lips collided. The kiss was short but deadly. The riot of emotions pumping through her when Kegen pulled away far too soon, were almost too much. The barest touch of his lips against hers and she forgot herself. She opened her mouth to ask why he pulled away, but he must have known what she was going to say.

"Any more than that and Rev will be listening to you moaning two seconds after I get you up on the counter. I'm trying to be a gentleman here, but once you get near me and start touching, all of my good intentions fly out the window."

"Well, we wouldn't want that to happen," she smirked. "I guess I'll have a lonely night without you then."

"You can stay here with me but it might be not as restful or fun. He needs his pain meds every few hours and I'm supposed to watch him. He hit his head when he went down too. They said he wasn't concussed but erred on the side of *better safe than sorry.*"

"I understand. I've got a big day tomorrow anyway. A couple of conference calls are scheduled for the afternoon. Need my wits about me."

Kegen took her hand as they walked into the living room. Stopping where Rev was passed out on the couch, she bent and gave him a peck on the cheek. He grunted and attempted to roll over, jerking himself awake when his injured leg didn't go with him. "Fuck, that hurts."

Marlowe grimaced. It looked painful. His ankle was swollen and turning an interesting shade of red. There was no way Rev was going anywhere without help. And here she was hoping Kegen would walk her home and she'd get another kiss. That wasn't going to happen. "I'll let you take care of him." She kissed Kegen on the cheek, stepping away before he could stop her. "Feel better, Rev."

Kegen nodded then moved toward his brother, holding out a hand for him to take. "Let's get you to bed, man. It's got be a lot more comfortable there than on the couch." Kegen heard the soft snick of the door as Marlowe left. He knew she would. She told him as much, but a part of him hoped she would stay a little longer.

It was best if he ignored the sense of loss filling him. At least for now. He had a whiny little brother to take care of first.

He felt shitty when he realized he'd forgotten the dinner plans they made. The dinner she cut out of work early to make and he would bet created a beautiful setting for the evening too. Family came first and like the drama queen his brother was, Rev milked getting hurt for all it was worth. Kegen didn't doubt it hurt like hell, but Rev was a lot tougher and had gotten hurt worse than the seriously sprained ankle he was suffering from now.

It didn't help matters that Kegen had to deal with the pretty client's demands that she go with them to the hospital. To him, it wasn't necessary but Rev thought otherwise. Rev convinced Kegen it was the right thing to do since she was the reason he was hurt. Flawed logic, but he didn't expect anything less from his younger brother.

Kegen relented and agreed to let her come along right about the time she said she needed to call her husband to let him know where she would be. Kegen put his foot down then, pissing her off royally.

Luckily, Quin stepped in to save the day. He pulled her aside, reminding her she was with her co-workers and that maybe it wasn't the best idea in the world. Explaining why she was going to the hospital with the man she spent the better part of the day flirting with wasn't going to be easy or go over well, no matter how many times she said she and her husband had an open marriage.

Once they got to the hospital and into the waiting room, Rev forgot all about the client. If the swarm of nurses were any indication, the man was definitely going to be busy the next couple of months. Though there was the one nurse, the one actually assigned to him, that wouldn't give Rev the time of day. It was the one bright spot in Kegen's otherwise shitty afternoon.

Which brought his thoughts back to Marlowe. She was the best part of his day. Waking up with her in the morning. Seeing her sleep mussed and curled up against him before he regretfully got out of bed. He thought about her constantly while at work. Wondering if she missed him like he missed her. Thinking about when he would see her again. What he wouldn't give to go some place where no one could find them. To lock themselves away from the world where he could tell her he was falling in love with her more each day.

He understood now why Quin did what he did with Laurel, keeping her to himself these past few months.

"Kegen!" Rev snapped his fingers a couple of times before grabbing his hand. "Dude, I've been sitting here trying to get your attention for a couple of minutes. Where the hell did you just go?"

Kegen shook his head. "Nowhere. Let's go you lazy bum."

"You have to move out of my way dipshit and don't lie to me. I know you were thinking about Marlowe."

Kegen stepped to the side to give his brother space to swing his legs around. "So what if I was. It isn't a crime to think about the woman you're involved with."

Rev wobbled as he stood. Kegen reached out to steady him. The damn coffee table was in the way and Rev couldn't move without hurting himself more. Kegen set his foot against the wood and shoved. With more room to maneuver, he moved next to his brother's bad side, hooking his arm around his waist.

They slowly walked to the side of the house where their rooms were located. Both silent and lost in their thoughts. Kegen got Rev to his room and situated him on the bed, as he turned, Rev caught his arm. "You can go over there and be with her. I'll be fine on my own."

Damn, he was tempted to do what Rev said. "Nah, she has work to do. Besides, I'm not giving you a reason to tattle on me. Mom is going to flip her lid when she finds out you got hurt trying to impress a married woman. I won't be your scapegoat."

Rev chuckled but Kegen could hear the edge of pain in his voice. "Dick."

"Give me a minute and I'll get your pain meds." On the way out of the room, Kegen heard his phone beep. Digging it out of his pocket again, he checked his messages. There was a new message from Quin. "Shit," he grumbled.

Reaching into the fridge, he grabbed a bottle of water, found the pain meds he had tossed on the counter earlier, and made his way back to his brother.

Rev was lying perfectly still when Kegen walked into the room. "What's up?" he asked, never opening his eyes.

Kegen snorted. "Mom and Dad are on their way home from the trip. Seems someone at the hospital called to schedule a time for a follow up and they called Mom. You still have her down as your contact."

Rev groaned. "Shit."

With their parents coming back and Rev being hurt, Kegen didn't think he'd be getting much of a chance to see Marlowe anytime soon.

Opening the bottle of water, he handed it to his brother along with two pills. "Numb the pain and rest. You're gonna need it with Mom hovering around. Call me if you need me."

Kegen spun away. He was going to need some rest too. Cleaning up and locking the house, he headed to bed. He needed to find a way to see Marlowe. With his parents on the way, there was no way he was going to make it not seeing her.

Chapter Nine

The loud rumble and squeaking breaks of something pretty damn big drew Marlowe to the front window. The biggest RV she had ever seen pulled up in front of Kegen and Rev's place, not stopping until it was blocking the guys' trucks and her car in.

"What the fuck?" Whipping the front door open, she was seconds from telling the asshole to move when Kegen came loping out of his house.

His black hair was slicked back and wet. He'd forgotten his shirt and, for the love of god, his jeans were riding dangerously snug and low. Instant need pulsed through her at the sight. Her panties flooded with arousal. Her nipples pulled tight and pushed against the white lace of her demi-bra. Oh God, the man was sex personified.

"Dad, you can't park there."

Dad! Marlowe backed up; hoping none of them saw her. She pressed her back to her door as she groped for the handle.

Please don't see me. Please don't see me. Please don't see me.

Luckily for her, they didn't. Her hand finally landed on the handle and as she turned it, a woman who looked to be around fifty came flying around the front of the RV, stopping her from retreating. Marlowe's curiosity about the situation overrode all of her common sense along with the need for escape.

"Where is my baby?" She kept moving past Kegen and went straight into the house.

"You know the way Mom. In his room still," he called out. He didn't even have to raise his voice much. Their voices traveled to her ears easily in the quiet of the morning.

Kegen's dad stepped down from the RV, shut the door and hugged his son. "How's he doing?"

"He's fine Dad. It's just a bad sprain. You guys didn't need to cut your trip short because of it."

The older man chuckled. "Like your mother would ever do that. She talks a good game, but I never believed a word of that *you're on your own* speech she gave you boys. Now what were you saying when I pulled up?"

"You can't park there, Dad. You're blocking in my neighbor." His hand lifted and gestured toward where Marlowe stood rooted to the spot. Her mind was screaming at her to go in and shut the door, but her body wasn't listening. Kegen's gaze landed on her. The corner of his mouth curved up and before she knew it, he was walking toward her with his Dad following.

The similarities between the men were uncanny. It made perfect sense since the man was his father, but still—they looked so much alike. Kegen's dad sported the same black hair but sprinkled with gray and cut stylishly short. He was tall, had a tapered waist and broad shoulders like all three of his sons. The most shocking thing for her was how surprisingly fit he looked for a man who had to be in his mid to late fifties.

If this was an indication of how Kegen would look when he was older, she heartily approved. As the men approached, she couldn't help but smooth down the knee length pencil skirt she was wearing. She adjusted the jacket that went with, dropping her head to check to see if there were any stray hairs or pieces of lint. By the time she looked back up, Kegen in all his manly goodness was standing in front of her. He leaned in to kiss her, aiming straight for her lips but at the last second kissed her on the cheek.

Well, that's disappointing. "Morning, Kegen. I see you have company."

He looked behind him at his dad, shook his head and focused on her again. "Yeah, I'll get him to move that behemoth so you can get your car out. Mom was in a bit of a hurry to check on Rev."

"Oh, is he worse than last night?"

"Nope, but he is the baby. Needs special coddling." Marlowe laughed and Kegen's dad cleared his throat. "Sorry. Marlowe this is my dad, Brendon Ferris. Dad, this is Marlowe Scott, my neighbor."

So, he wants to introduce me as just his neighbor. Okay. I can play that game. Marlowe held out her hand, putting her most dazzling smile on her face. "Nice to meet you, Mr. Ferris."

"It's nice to meet you too, Marlowe. Connie was a little anxious to make sure Revlin was okay. We drove all night to get back here after we got the call from the hospital." He looked at Kegen, eyebrow raised, a slight frown on his face. Marlowe snorted, then quickly cleared her throat to try and mask the sound.

Kegen let out an exasperated breath. "Dad, it's just a sprain and he didn't even do it jumping. He tripped, while flirting!" His voice raised on the last part.

Marlowe's eyebrows shot up. She had never heard Kegen talk like that. "Okay then. Well, I'm sure Rev will be just fine now that you guys are here to help out." Glancing at her watch, she noted she didn't have nearly as much time as she thought she did. "Oh my! I really do need to get going. I have a lot to do to prep for those conference calls later."

"Let me back the RV up then. Again, it was nice to meet you. The boys will have to have you over sometime this week while we're staying here."

It was Kegen's turn to have his eyebrows shoot up, though his was in apparent surprise. Marlowe chuckled at the panicked look on his face. "You're staying here? Dad," he called out, but his father had already jogged off.

Marlowe moved, opened her door, grabbed her keys and briefcase off the entry table then locked the house. All while Kegen just stood there. Brooding.

Skirting around Kegen, she headed for her car. She was irritated about not getting a proper kiss and being introduced as just the neighbor. And just as irritated at being irritated about those things.

Sliding into the seat of her car, she started it up, plugged in her phone, and was in the middle of finding a good song when there was a tap on her window.

She hit the button and waited for it to go down all of the way. "Is there something I can help you with?"

Kegen leaned in slightly. "Sorry about them blocking you in."

"Don't worry about it, Kegen. I'm sure your mom was just in a hurry to check on your brother. I hear some parents are like that."

He ran his fingers through his hair and all she could think about was doing the same. Unlike the last time she did it, she wouldn't do it now. The RV started up behind her, a horrible beeping noise announcing to the neighborhood that it was backing up.

"Good luck with the parents staying with you. If you need an escape and aren't afraid to let them know we're more than just *neighbors*, you know where I live."

"Wait a minute." He wrapped his hand around the back of her neck and was pulling her toward him when his dad honked the RV's horn. The loud jingly tune caused her to jump in her seat, dislodging his hand. "Jesus, a guy can't catch a break," he grumbled.

"Probably for the best since they would want to know why you're kissing your *neighbor*." She stuck the car into reverse. "I guess I'll see you whenever." Popping the emergency brake she slowly rolled back, giving Kegen time to step away.

"Marlowe," he called after her.

She refused to look at him and drove off. It was quite possible she was a little more ticked off about being introduced as a neighbor than she would like to admit.

Kegen stepped back and watched Marlowe drive away. Damn, he didn't want to let her go.

Last night had been miserable without her. Whenever Rev woke up, Kegen would reach for Marlowe, disappointment filling him each time he realized she wasn't there.

He was dying to kiss her. Hold her in his arms. Stroke his hands down her back until he had two luscious handfuls of her ass.

Kegen groaned, but this time not in pleasure. His dad following him had not been in his plans. Quite honestly, he'd forgotten about him the second Kegen had seen Marlowe. When he took off to her place, he for sure thought the old man would head inside to check on the giant baby of the family. Instead, he'd fucked up by introducing her as his neighbor and not his girlfriend. But he didn't think it was the best way to spring it on his parents that he was dating her.

Sullenly, Kegen walked back to his driveway. His dad pulled the RV back in its original spot and hopped out again.

"Nice girl," his dad commented nonchalantly.

"Yep." It was all he was going to say. The last thing he wanted at the moment was to be interrogated by his father. He felt his dad's gaze on him, studying him. Kegen tried to keep a blank expression on his face and was finding it hard. Just like his damn dick. That prim and proper outfit she had on drove him nuts. It was so business-like and not her at all.

Damn, she was probably wearing something filmy and tiny underneath it. Kegen turned back toward the house. He really didn't need his dad noticing the hard-on in his pants. Back inside, Kegen headed straight for his room and grabbed a shirt. Slipping it over his head, he walked back out into the living room, nearly running over his dad. It seemed he wasn't quite ready to drop the topic of Marlowe.

"I'm surprised we haven't seen her before, here or in town. Has she been living in that house long?"

"Over six months." He detoured into the kitchen, planting himself in front of the coffeemaker.

"I'll take a cup, son." His father leaned back against the counter, crossing his leanly muscled arms over his chest.

Kegen was always impressed that his dad remained fit, even after retirement a couple years ago.

Once his mom turned fifty, she retired from teaching and she and his dad spent a year learning to take it easy. Sleeping in late, going out with friends and not worrying about waking up early the next day.

They also spent that first year getting used to being around each other all of the time. There were times he and his brothers thought one parent would kill the other but they didn't.

This last year they started planning their cross-country travels. They both wanted to see the sights on their timeline. To have the freedom to do what they wanted, when they wanted.

They'd gone on a couple of trips close by, getting the feel of the new RV and learning to let him and his brothers live their lives. That was the most difficult thing for their mom. She didn't baby them, well she didn't baby Quin and him, but it came damn close.

When the coffeemaker sputtered, he filled a cup for himself and one for his dad. Handing it to him, he noticed the look on his dad's face. The crafty ole guy knew there was something going on. Kegen could tell by the glimmer lighting his eyes.

"Want to tell me about it? About her?"

"Nothing to tell, dad. Marlowe's our neighbor. She's been living here for a bit and we've, Rev and I, all became friends. I like her. She's nice."

"Mhmm and…"

Shit. First he kept his mouth shut and then he couldn't shut the hell up. His dad would definitely know something was up. That wouldn't stop him from trying to convince his dad otherwise. Not until the time was right. "And nothing." Kegen moved to the dining table and sat down. It was all in an effort to not have to look his dad in the eyes and to give even more away.

"Nothing my ass. I saw you leaning into her car. I bet if I hadn't honked that silly ass horn you would still have your lips locked on hers."

Yeah, he would have. "I wasn't kissing her."

"But you were trying to." His dad grinned and sat down across from him.

Kegen felt a blush rush to his cheeks. In his head, he knew he was a grown man, but being caught by your dad trying to kiss a girl was still a little embarrassing. He chose not to answer one-way or the other. His dad knew he was right. No need to let him gloat about it.

His dad was about to say something more when his mom came into the kitchen. "That boy! I just don't know what to do with him." She grabbed a cup, filled it with coffee then rooted around in his fridge for the creamer. They made sure they kept some just for her. After fixing her coffee how she liked it, she joined Kegen and his dad at the table. "Why didn't you stop him Kegen?"

Kegen sat back in surprise. "Stop him from doing what? Making an ass out of himself by tripping over his own equipment or from flirting with a married woman?"

"She was married? Oh dear." She looked at his dad, placing her hand on his arm. "Brendon, we really need to do something about Revlin. This reckless behavior has gone on far too long. He's going to get caught up in something too big to handle soon and you don't have enough friends on the police force to get him out of it."

Kegen's dad chuckled. "Connie, he's a grown man. He'll figure it out and you shouldn't expect Kegen or Quin to be the ones to stop him from messing up. Quin is busy, hopefully, convincing Laurel to marry him." His dad shot him a sly look and Kegen's stomach plummeted. "And Kegen has his hands full with his cute new neighbor, Marlowe. I'm thinking he's pretty smitten with her since he all but forgot about me. I think that's the girl he's been seeing these past few months."

"Way to throw me under the RV, Dad," Kegen mumbled.

"Anytime, son." His dad grinned and sipped his coffee. Kegen's mom whipped her head in Kegen's direction.

"Your neighbor?" she asked, surprise lifting her voice. "I don't know whether to be happy you've found someone or terrified about what will happen when you break up. Just don't go breaking her heart. No one wants a repeat of what happened with that girl that used to live behind us. She was so love-struck with you boys. I have to say, those flowers she sent you at school were very pretty though."

The heat on Kegen's cheeks intensified. "That was in high school, Mom. I'm an adult now and so is Marlowe. I promise we'll behave."

His dad snorted and Kegen cut him a look. "That didn't look like you were behaving to me. Kegen was trying to get a smooch out of her." His dad made horrible kissing noises toward his mom. She, in turn, started giggling and leaned in for a kiss.

Kegen rolled his eyes and pushed away from the table as his parents chuckled behind his back. That right there was why he didn't want his parents knowing about him and Marlowe yet. Endless teasing from his brothers was one thing. From his parents... he would never recover from it.

Rinsing his coffee cup out, he took a breath and turned toward his parents. "Dad, I'll need you to move the RV so I can get my truck out. I'm heading into work since you and mom are here to look after Rev." He strode out of the room, not wanting to wait for their reply, or to see what other embarrassing things they were doing.

In his room, he shut and locked his door. Not that he expected anyone to follow him. He just needed a couple minutes alone to gather his thoughts. How the hell was he supposed to see Marlowe now that his parents were there? They would never get a moment alone.

Shit. Maybe he would come up with something between now and when he drove home after work.

Heading to the closet, he pulled a medium-sized rucksack out. Filling it with a change of clothes and a few essential hygiene items so he could clean up before heading home.

He slung it onto his shoulder, walked out of his room and into the hallway.

Looking toward his brother's room, he made the last minute decision to check in on Rev. Peeking in, he found him fast asleep, or at least that's how it looked. Shrugging, Kegen figured he would just text Rev later to see how it was going.

Expecting to see his mom, Kegen was surprised when she wasn't out in the living room waiting to pounce on him. She never missed an opportunity to find out about the women her sons dated. He was lucky to hold her off as long as he had.

She always wanted to know all of the stats and if the woman of the moment was *The One*. Heading out the front door, he saw his Mom in the RV as his Dad stood next to Kegen's truck. He approached the vehicle warily.

"Your mom and I are going to drive the RV home then come back over in the car. Your brother is asleep so he shouldn't need us for a bit."

"I saw. I checked in on him."

"Your mom said to make sure you're home on time tonight. Dinner will be ready around six."

"Alright, Pop." Kegen rounded the front of the truck then opened the driver's side door. Tossing the bag in first, he climbed inside. He glanced at his dad through the passenger window. His Dad was grinning and Kegen knew being told to be home on time wasn't the only thing his Mom wanted. He pressed the button to put the window down.

"Your Mom said to invite Marlowe over for dinner. It's the neighborly thing to do."

"She may have plans," Kegen hedged. He wasn't quite sure inviting Marlowe over was a good idea. He still hadn't talked to her about them. Bringing her over would put both of them in the hot seat.

"But you don't know? Can't hurt to ask, unless you aren't that serious about her and are just playing around. Maybe you feel a need to take out a restraining order. Missed all of that legal mumbo-jumbo stuff from that incident in high school."

Kegen shook his head. "Very funny," he said flatly. "I'll try to get hold of her, but I'm not promising anything. Make sure Mom knows that."

Kegen's dad winked then nodded. He turned and Kegen watched as he climbed up in the RV. He could see his parents talking animatedly then heard the rumble of the monster RV start up. As they pulled away, Kegen wondered if he had time to stop by Whispers.

Glancing at the dashboard clock, he grinned like it idiot. It wasn't like Quin was expecting him in today anyway.

Chapter Ten

A knock on Marlowe's door brought her head up and out of the numbers swimming in front of her face. She really needed to get Steph in and have her look over everything. You would never know it by looking at her, but Steph was a freaking math wiz.

"Come in," she called out when the knock sounded again.

Her employee, Monica, pushed the door open. Her eyes were wide and she kept glancing furtively over her shoulder. "There's someone here to see you, Ms. Scott."

The girl looked over her shoulder again and gasped. "Sir, I asked you to wait out front. Only employees are allowed back here."

A deep chuckled echoed down the hall that lead back to Marlowe's office. She would recognize that sound anywhere. Marlowe couldn't help the smile that formed on her lips. "It's okay, Monica. Thank you."

"Yes ma'am." The girl stepped aside as Kegen filled the doorway. Marlowe noticed Monica's gaze trailed down the back of Kegen, snagging on his ass. She really couldn't blame the girl for staring. He was as handsome as ever. He still wore the jeans he'd had on that morning but had thrown on a black Chute Shack t-shirt. The material stretched across his broad shoulders, highlighting the strength underneath. Her fingers itched to push his shirt up and smooth over his skin.

She couldn't find it in her to still be upset about the morning. Time away from the situation brought clarity. Maybe his parents didn't know they were dating in the first place. She surely wouldn't want to spring that on her Dad while standing on that person's front porch.

Kegen turned his head and smiled at the poor besotted girl. "Ms. Scott is going to be busy for a little bit, Monica. Please make sure she isn't disturbed." He stepped through the door and shut it on the girl's shocked face.

Marlowe laughed. "You've traumatized her, I'm sure."

Kegen's eyes twinkled with amusement. "She probably thinks I'm Rev and is wondering why I'm not flirting with her. That *is* the girl he was talking about the other day, right?"

Marlowe snorted. "Yes, she's the one. He is a bit of a slut. He hit on her and the other girl training that morning. How is he anyway? Your parents waiting on him hand and foot?" An indecipherable look came over Kegen's face at the mention of his parents. She got up from her chair, concern overriding any thrill she felt at having him stop in unexpectedly. Taking his hand, she pulled him to the chair in front of her desk and forced him to sit. "What's wrong? Are they okay? Is Rev okay? He didn't injure his foot even more, did he?"

Kegen reached out when she went to step away, grabbing her around the waist. He pulled her until she was sitting in his lap, turning her so her legs were dangling over the arm of the chair. "Nothing is wrong. Everyone is fine. Rev is as injured now as he was last night."

"Then why the weird look when I mentioned your parents?"

"You're awfully perceptive."

Marlowe shrugged. She was perceptive because she was way too into him.

"I'm sorry I didn't introduce you to my dad as my girlfriend."

"Oh!" She squirmed a little on his lap. Her world didn't feel like it was falling apart because he called her that. But the strange giddy feeling she felt was unfamiliar.

Kegen studied her face. Everywhere he looked, it felt like a caress. "Is that a good 'oh' or bad 'oh'?"

"It isn't a bad 'oh'. It's more of a surprised 'oh'."

"You didn't think we were at that point?"

"I wasn't sure what point you were at."

He nodded. "Okay. There did seem to be an unspoken agreement about not talking about it. I want to change that. I consider you to be my girlfriend."

"O-okay." She could have smacked herself at the stutter. Her pulse was out of control as her brain read into what he was saying.

He was looking at her as if he was waiting for her to say something else. She would if she could figure out what she was supposed to say.

Thankfully, he took mercy on her. "Do you consider me to be your boyfriend?"

Marlowe giggled at the term boyfriend. She was twenty-eight. Could you really call the guy you were seeing your *boyfriend* when you were that age?

"What's so funny, Peaches?"

"It just sounds strange to me. I don't think I've ever called a man I dated my boyfriend."

"Well, I want to be. Among other things," he grunted, before nuzzling his lips against the sensitive skin behind her ear, sending a thrilling tingle down her spine.

"Oh, I can handle that," she muttered.

His hot breath wafted across her neck as he proceeded to nibble on her. She tilted her head to give him more access. As he worked his way up her neck, nipping and licking her ear, he cupped her face with one hand and turned her head toward him. He kissed her, his tongue invading her mouth as his fingers tangled in her hair. She got lost in the seductive drug of his lips against hers.

Kegen broke the kiss and she felt his smile against her lips. "You taste so good."

Marlowe snuggled closer to him, letting her head fall onto his shoulder. Closing her eyes, she placed a hand on his chest, soaking up the feel of him. His heart beat steadily. His breathing was relaxed. Kegen's arms came around her, comforting and secure. She could easily fall asleep sitting like that.

Kegen's deep voice rumbled under her. "I should wake up every day with you in my arms."

"It is rather nice." she quipped.

"I missed you last night."

"I missed you too."

They didn't say anything more. Just sat in silence. Contentment rolled off Kegen as he stroked her back in small lazy circles. Unfortunately, her office phone started ringing, breaking the spell that had woven around them. "Sorry." She scrambled off his lap. Thanks to her short stature and the placement of the phone on the far corner, she had to stretch across the desk to answer it, placing her ass in the air. "Hello?"

Kegen stood up behind her mumbling something. She turned her head to look at him with questioning eyes. The corner of his mouth kicked up in a devilish smile. He palmed her ass, squeezing it and groaned. Pulling her back slightly, he leaned over her, and nipped her shoulder. A shudder raced down her spine causing her to press into his groin even more.

"I'm going to have to call you back, Mr. Finnegan, I need to finish up with a client." She paused and tried to listen to what Drake Finnegan was saying, but it wasn't working. Kegen ground his erection against her, gripping her hips firmly in the process. All she could think about doing was hiking her skirt up and spreading her thighs. "Thanks," she mumbled. She tossed the phone toward the cradle and hoped she made it.

A moan ripped free from her throat. "You're killing me, Kegen."

"You aren't the only one dying," he growled. "That call important?"

"Yeah. Distributer. Trying to…oh god…get on board." Kegen slowly pumped his hips against her. His erection hard and insistent. Arousal flooded her panties and she absently wondered if cotton would have absorbed better than the flimsy lace she had on.

He nipped her earlobe then laved away the pain. "I should let you get going then." He released her hips, stroking them as he stepped back.

Marlowe spun around. "Seriously?" How could he leave her like this? Her gaze dropped to his crotch. "How can you leave like *that*?" She pointed to his erection clearly outlined by his jeans. She wanted to run her hands along the length, using the friction of the jeans to arouse him further. She knew he would be naked underneath. She would have a field day touching and fondling him.

Licking her lips, she stepped toward him. Snagging his shirt, she pushed him back into the chair and dropped to her knees in front of him.

Kegen leaned back, his black hair mussed around his face, his brown eyes filled with desire. "What do you have planned, Peaches?"

"Just a little morning pick-me-up. Something to start the day off right." Running her hands up his jean-clad legs; she curled her fingers through the belt loops in an attempt to keep him in one place. She knew if he wanted, he could break her hold, but she was sure he wouldn't.

Kegen nodded his head slightly.

"Good." Sliding her hands to the button, she unsnapped and unzipped his jeans, pushing the material to the sides. With one hand she reached inside, pulling his cock free. The hard flesh throbbed in her hand and she couldn't resist swiping her tongue over the head, licking away the drop of pre-cum beaded at the tiny slit.

Swirling her tongue around the engorged head, she watched for signs of his enjoyment. His thighs clenched, his breath came out ragged, his hands slid into her hair. Fisting the strands he tried to guide her lower. To make her suck in more of his length.

Marlowe took him fully into her mouth then, letting her lips settle down where her hand wrapped around the base. She worked him slow and steady, building on his pleasure. Soon she was hallowing out her cheeks as she rose and fell repeatedly over his length.

"Finger yourself, Marlowe. I want to see you come with my dick in your mouth."

With her free hand Marlowe hiked up her skirt, pulling it to the top of her thighs. Good thing she was wearing thigh high stockings. Shoving the scrap of lace she called underwear out of the way, she lightly ran her finger over her needy clit. The moan that broke free vibrated down Kegen's cock, pulling a guttural groan from him. She fingered herself faster as sensation tore through her.

Knowing she could pleasure Kegen like this, knowing she could derive her own pleasure like this empowered her. It let her show her love for him in the most primal way. She didn't expect anything in return as with past lovers. She wasn't trying to just get through it to get it over with. She was savoring it. Memorizing it. Loving it.

"Oh hell, Marlowe," he groaned. "Going to come. Come with me honey," he panted out.

Knowing he was so close she sucked harder, hungrier. Scraping her teeth delicately over his swollen flesh. A strangled cry burst from his lips as he filled her mouth. She drank him down with greedy gulp as her hot, wet fingers moved faster over her clit until she couldn't take it anymore. On a muffled moan she came, Kegen's erection still captured between her lips.

She sucked him gently, soothing his still hard flesh as shudders wracked his frame. His fingers loosened in her hair; the blissful moment over.

Before she had a chance to stand, he gathered her in his arms, placing her on his lap, and took her mouth. She was slightly shocked when he swept his tongue inside her mouth, having just swallowed his cum. He didn't seem to care.

He broke the kiss and leaned his forehead against hers. "Now that is the best pick-me-up I've ever had."

"I agree." Marlowe looked down at the tangled mess of her clothes. "Help me stand, please."

Kegen helped her up and as she straightened out her jacket, panties and skirt, he tucked himself back in his pants.

She walked around to the other side of her desk and grabbed a mint from her drawer. "What do you have going on tonight? Your parents are taking care of Rev, right?"

Kegen nodded.

"Come over after work. I'll cook you some dinner, we'll drink some wine and relax, then we can see where the night takes us."

Kegen's lips thinned. "I can't tonight. I've already been instructed to be home at six."

"Oh," she said feeling a little deflated. "Maybe another night then."

Kegen looked away. Marlowe thought it was strange when she noticed a slight blush race across his cheeks. He cleared his throat and looked back at her. "Mom wanted me to invite you to dinner tonight."

"Oh!" Well, that was a little surprising. She wasn't quite sure what to think about that. Did they talk about her this morning after Kegen and his dad went back inside? How weird would that be to sit around the table and talk about the woman you were seeing but wouldn't admit to?

"You don't have to come. She said it was the neighborly thing to do and I told my dad I would check with you to make her happy."

Marlowe frowned. "You don't want me to come over," she said it as a statement. It was certainly the vibe she was getting off him.

Kegen moved around the desk to stand in front of her. He pulled her into his arms. "I would love for you to come over. I just don't want my parents to scare you off. I want you completely crazy about me before you meet them."

"If I can put up with Rev, then I'm pretty sure I can handle your parents."

Kegen's gaze softened. "Don't say I didn't warn you. Don't worry about bringing anything over. If I know my mom, she'll have all the bases covered when it comes to the food. If you do feel the need to bring something, I wouldn't be against more of those cookies." He dropped a scorching kiss on her lips. Breaking apart, he released her and went straight for the door, swinging it open. "Have a great day, Marlowe. Go snag that new distributer."

A tiny flutter of nervousness took flight in her belly and it had nothing to do with her meetings later that day, but everything to do with making a good impression on Kegen's parents.

Chapter Eleven

Kegen pulled up at his house a little after six that night. Finding his parents' car parked in his usual spot next to Rev's truck, he sighed and looked toward Marlowe's place. He didn't think she would mind him using the spot so he pulled in next to her car.

Seconds after he turned the truck off, his phone buzzed snaring his attention. Plucking it out of the cup holder he checked it, finding two messages waiting for him.

Mom: *You're late. Get your butt home. We're ready to eat. Marlowe isn't here either.*

Kegen chuckled. Leave it to his mom to make him feel like he was sixteen again. He checked the second message.

Marlowe: *I'm not going to make it to dinner.*

A knot tightened in Kegen's chest. Did she have second thoughts about meeting his parents? After he left her at work, the idea of her meeting them grew on him more and more throughout the day.

Kegen: *Everything okay?*

Marlowe: *Yes. Just work. Stuff that needs to be done before tomorrow. Tell your parents I'm sorry.*

Kegen didn't like the disappointment that rolled through him. He was looking forward to seeing her. Climbing out of the truck, he went straight to her front door and knocked. Shoving his hands into his front pockets, he waited. It didn't take long for her to answer.

"Hey." Marlowe stood in front of him still wearing most of the starched up business suit from earlier. She'd taken the jacket off and stood in her bare feet, skirt and a cream camisole looking as beautiful as ever.

He fisted his hands in his pockets in an effort not to reach out and grab her. "Hey."

"I'm sorry, Kegen, I just can't make it tonight. The distributer I talked to this afternoon is interested, but he wants some figures and promotion ideas to see how we plan on advertising the line. He wants it tomorrow and I have to get it done."

Kegen just nodded his head. "Have you had anything to eat at all?"

She shook her head. "I'll get something when I'm done. I've got the figures done and am on a roll with the advertising. Another hour or two and I'll be able to relax. Please tell your mom thank you for the invitation. Maybe I'll get a chance to meet her some other time."

"I'm sure you will." His phone buzzed in his pocket. Pulling it out, he saw another message from his mom telling him to hurry up and stop playing kissy-face. He grunted and shoved the phone back in his pocket.

Reaching out, he captured Marlowe's hands and gently tugged her close to him. Lowering his face, he kissed her; sliding his tongue into her mouth when she gasped in surprise. Their tongues tangled and he was overwhelmed by the need going through him. Her slim body melted into him, breasts pressing into his chest. She rested her hands against his chest before sliding them up around his neck. Her fingers found purchase in his hair. He loved how she tugged and gripped his locks like she was afraid he would get away.

Marlowe was the one to break the kiss this time. She dropped back down onto flat feet, letting go of his hair at the same time. "Wow. You sure know how to kiss a girl."

"Thanks." His phone went off again, playing an upbeat tune from his pocket. "That's my mom. I guess I should get over there."

Marlowe stepped back, a look of disappointment on her face. "Yeah, I need to get back to work. Thanks for stopping by."

Kegen kissed her quickly. "Anytime. I'll see you later." He turned from the door and before he could step away, Marlowe grabbed his ass. "Hey, that's my butt."

"Yep and a nice one at that." She chuckled and closed the door.

Kegen jogged to his house. "I'm home," he announced once he went through the door.

His mom came out of the kitchen all smiles, which quickly faded. "No Marlowe?"

He shared the disappointment. "No, she has work to do. I'll take her some food after we eat. I'm sure she'll forget. She's knee deep in advertising and promotional ideas"

Rev piped up from the dining room. "Yeah, she definitely will."

Kegen and his mom joined Rev and their dad in the dining room. Rev had his leg propped up on a chair. Their mom looked between Kegen and Rev, finally letting her gaze rest on Rev. "You know this about her?"

Kegen moved around to the other side of the table and sat down. It would be interesting to see how Rev handled this.

"Well, yeah. We are friends. I know she gets pretty focused when it comes to something for the boutique." Rev shrugged.

"You two aren't both dating her, are you?" Their mom sat down next to their dad and Kegen was bowled over by a sense of déjà vu. The only one missing was Quin, but the lucky bastard was with his fiancée no doubt.

"To answer your question, no, we both aren't dating her. She isn't that kind of woman. I'm pretty certain she thinks of Rev just like Laurel thinks of him… an annoying little shit."

"Dick," Rev said before throwing a piece of broccoli at him.

"Revlin Ferris, you do not throw food at your brother!" Their mother's stern reprimand made Kegen laugh. She turned her head toward him—frown on her face. "Don't you start either. And don't use foul language."

The three men around the table laughed, then they all dug into dinner. After they were done eating, Kegen helped his mom clear the table while his dad helped Rev move back to his bedroom. Turning to bring the last of the plates over to the counter, his mother held out her empty hand. He handed them to her and she handed him a plate full of food covered in plastic wrap. "Take this to your girlfriend."

He kissed her on the cheek before taking the plate from her. "Thanks, Mom."

"Be back before midnight, you have work tomorrow and I'm sure she does as well."

Kegen left the house and made his way over to Marlowe's. He knocked on the door and waited. When she answered this time, she was wearing fuzzy animal print pajama bottoms, matching fuzzy socks and a pink tank top. "Nice outfit."

She looked down then back up. "I like it. Nice and warm and fuzzy. Perfect after a long day."

"Mom sent over some food." He held out the plate to her. When she went to take it he leaned in and kissed her, holding the food away. "You get your work done?"

"Yes. Now may I the food? I'm starving. I was just looking to see if I had anything quick and easy to make. FYI, I don't."

"Good thing I stopped by then." He grinned, pleased with himself for mentioning to his mom about bringing food over.

"Let me grab a hoodie and we can sit on the front porch while I eat. It's too pretty of a night and I didn't get to spend much time outside breathing fresh air today."

"Sounds good. How about that glass of wine we keep talking about having?"

The corners of her mouth lifted into a beautiful smile. "That would be nice. I'll meet you out front."

A couple of minutes later, Marlowe came out of the house carrying a fork and two glasses of wine. She sat down in the open chair and handed him a glass, then took the food from his hands. He let her eat, waiting until she was finished and set the plate on the ground.

"That was delicious. Tell your mother thank you for the food." She canted her head and looked at him out of the corner of her eyes. "And thank you for mentioning it to her. I'm sure she wouldn't' have known I hadn't eaten unless you'd said something."

"Anytime, but hopefully you'll be over when there's another offer of dinner."

"I hope so too." She leaned back in her chair, took a sip of her wine and breathed out a contented breath. She reached for his hand and threaded their fingers together. "So, how was your day?"

Kegen squeezed her hand lightly, liking how it felt twined with his. "Good. We didn't jump today. We're working out the logistics of the Utah jump for next month. Who's going. Who's staying. Flying or driving? Stuff like that. How did yours go after I left?"

"Good. Busy. You know about the distributer from the call this morning. Got some new samples of men's clothing coming in. Looked into hiring another girl for the afternoon and shopped website designers. I also managed to get Steph on the hook to look over the financials."

Kegen chuckled. He just couldn't imagine Steph sitting down working over numbers, but you never knew about a person. "I have to admit, I can't see her doing that."

Marlowe turned her head toward him and smiled. "Her image is definitely deceiving. She's a math wiz. She's been running the figures and finances for her dad's construction projects for years."

"That's cool." It hit him then that this was the perfect opportunity to ask Marlowe more about her parents. "What does your dad do?"

Marlowe stiffened slightly, then relaxed. "He's ex-military. Right now he's on a fishing trip with some buddies, I think."

"You think? You don't know." Kegen heard the surprise in his voice. How did someone not know what his or her parents were up to? Kegen and his brothers were always well informed about their parents' schedule and activities. They were close like that.

"Like I told you before, we don't really talk. After my Mom died, my dad didn't know what to do with me. Hell, he didn't know what to do with me before she passed away. I wasn't the boy he had hoped for, and he and mom never had any more kids."

"I'm sorry, Marlowe."

She waved his sympathetic comment away. "It isn't a big deal. At this point, I'm used to it."

They sat in silence for a bit. He didn't know what was going through her mind, but he was blown away learning she didn't have the kind of relationship he had with his parents. He always figured he would fall for someone that thought love and family were the most important things in life. As long as you had both, then everything else was icing.

"Kinda threw you for a loop, didn't it?" she said quietly into the night.

Kegen set his glass of wine down on the table next to him. "Yeah. I know not everyone has a family like mine. We're close knit and in each other's back pocket for the most part. It's still a little shocking to hear others didn't grow up like that. I couldn't imagine what it would be like growing up without one of my parents around."

"Try either around."

"What?" Now that was a confusing statement.

"Once mom was gone, he had no clue what to do with a girl on the brink of her teen years. He decided the best thing for me was private schools and summer camps. It let him keep doing what he was doing and he didn't have to worry about me. It also meant I wasn't around as a reminder of my mother and all that he had lost. He took her death horribly."

"But didn't you as well? Wouldn't he want to be there to make sure you were okay?"

"I don't think it ever crossed his mind. I was twelve and growing more distant. I would hole up in my room, listen to music and be a pre-teen with too many new hormones coursing through me."

"That isn't an excuse though. He should have been there. Look at Rev. He's barely hurt and my parents cancelled their trip and have basically moved in." Kegen wanted to groan at the intrusion of them but, hearing what Marlowe said, he knew he was lucky they would do such a thing. "How did she die, if you don't mind me asking?"

"Car accident. She was coming home from some military wives' meeting; it was raining terribly, a truck skid through a red light hitting her broadside. Death was instantaneous, thankfully."

Kegen tugged on Marlowe's hand and pulled her over to him, settling her on his lap. The way she talked, so matter of fact and emotionless, killed him. He couldn't imagine having to go through the death of a parent then be shoved away by the other parent at such a young age.

Marlowe snuggled into his chest as he wrapped his arms around her. She sighed, "You would think I wouldn't be as well adjusted as I am with all of that shit happening so young. At one time, Steph decided I had commitment issues."

The comment pricked at something in the back of his mind, triggering a memory. Her surprise when he called her his girlfriend. The comment that she never called a man she was seeing a boyfriend. "You don't?"

"Maybe at one time. I used to be afraid people would leave me so I refused to make friends at the school I went to. Then my second year there, I met Steph and she bullied her way into my life. I quit being so scared and we've been friends ever since. She was and still is my rock. She helped me not go down that dark rabbit hole of depression and to learn to take life as it came and do the things I love. I'm really okay, Kegen. I can tell you're worried."

"I am. I just can't imagine going through all of that. Being on your own and not having family support."

"Ah, but I had Steph and her family. I went home with her on holidays and breaks. Did you know she has five older brothers and they're all hot? I had such crushes on them growing up." She leaned away from him, smiled and winked.

"No, I didn't know that," Kegen growled out.

"Don't worry, Kegen, I like you much better than I ever did them. Which is saying a lot." She kissed his cheek then pushed out of his arms to stand in front of him. "Thanks for bringing the food."

"Is this your way of telling me to go home?" He shoved out of the chair.

Leaning over, she picked up the plate and both of their wine glasses. "For now. I'm tired and have an early morning. I'm sure you have work tomorrow as well." She handed the plate to him.

"You know one of these days we're going to get more than just an evening or a few stolen moments together."

"I live for that day but, until then, give me a kiss and wish me a goodnight, Kegen."

Kegen plucked the glasses from her hands and set them and the empty plate on the side table. He cupped her face, determined to keep his hands there and only there. It was far too easy to get lost in touching her.

The desire swimming in the depths of her eyes almost made him cave. He was stronger than the temptation but just barely. He skimmed his lips over hers, keeping the pressure light, dragging out the pleasure for both of them. Marlowe moaned and tried to take the kiss deeper.

With as much control as possible, he let go of her face, grabbed the plate, and started back across the yard. "Sweet dreams, Marlowe. I'll see you tomorrow. That's a promise."

Chapter Twelve

The next few days followed much like Monday. Kegen was able to see Marlowe before she took off to work. Showing up at her door minutes before she rushed out of it. Kissing her senseless and starting his day off with a bang.

During the day, they would text back and forth. Silly little things like *how was your day* or *what are you doing*. He even got off a *what are you wearing* text followed by *send pictures* when she told him she and some of her friends were having a lingerie party.

Explaining to him that they had gotten in a new shipment for the boutique and were drinking wine and trying on outfits while the store was closed. He offered to come help when she sent a picture of herself wearing a zebra print mesh teddy but was told no.

His parents moved back to their own house Thursday morning, telling Rev it was time for him to get up and get moving. To do the physical therapy recommended by the doctor and get back to normal. But with fewer shenanigans, please.

Kegen was thankful since it meant he got to sleep in his own bed again, having slept on the couch while his parents took his room. It wasn't horribly uncomfortable but the damn thing wasn't built for night after night of restless tossing and turning.

Even though they went home, that still didn't stop them from being at his house at all hours of the day and dinnertime, including Thursday night.

Marlowe had yet to come over, much to everyone's disappointment, working late every night. The distributer was on board with her plans, contracts were signed and a shifting of merchandise was taking place late into the evenings after the store closed.

No matter what time she got home, he would go over and they would spend a couple minutes or, if they were lucky, a couple hours together on her front porch unwinding from the day. Just checking in with each other and getting some much needed physical and emotional support they hadn't been able to find with anyone else.

Kegen depended on her and that time together. It allowed him to clear his mind of all things skydiving related.

Looking around the break area outside the hanger, he made sure nothing was left on the ground from lunch. Sometimes the clients thought the Shack crew was there to cater to their every whim, including picking up after them. Thankfully, this group wasn't turning out to be like some of their more demanding clientele. Walking into the hanger through the large bay door, he smiled and nodded to the group milling about just inside. Crossing the room, he made his way to the corner where they kept couches, a large screen television, DVD player and some video games, for the rare down times.

Kegen passed Rev, who insisted on hobbling into work with him, sitting in Quin's office flirting harmlessly with fellow jumpmaster Charity. It was good to see Rev back to his jovial, flirtatious manner.

Quin obliviously walked by him talking on his cell.

Kegen could only guess that he was making plans with their parents for that evening to let them know about the engagement.

According to Quin, Laurel was talking about waiting a year to get married. Quin knew if he involved their Mom sooner rather than later, she could get the ball rolling and Quin would get Laurel down the aisle on his accelerated timeline.

Plopping down on the couch, Kegen leaned back and took stock of what he wanted in life. He loved his job. The skydiving business was flourishing with more people scheduling jumps now that they were rolling into Spring. He was on the home ownership path with his brother, but at some point that would have to change. They both couldn't live there once they decided to settle down with someone.

Kegen's thoughts drifted to Marlowe. He could definitely see himself settling down and moving in with her. Maybe get married after a few years. Have a couple of kids eventually. She was perfect for him. Driven. Independent. Smart. Not to mention sexy, funny, attentive and attuned to his thoughts. It was also an added bonus that he would still be living next door to his brother.

Glancing at the Shack's clock, he noticed it was going on to one-thirty. Pulling his phone out of his pocket, he tossed it back and forth before deciding to text her. He didn't remember her saying she had any meetings scheduled for the day. Hopefully, he could catch her in the office.

Kegen: *Whatcha doing?*

Kegen sent up a prayer hoping she would respond. His emotions were a little all over the place at the moment and he really needed her to ground him.

The more time they spent together, the more he realized he had drifted past liking her fondly to full blown fallen in love.

Kegen breathed a sigh of relief when Marlowe's response came swiftly.

Marlowe: *Just finished up lunch. Going to head out onto the floor and see how things are going. I'm hoping to leave early today. What are you up to?*

Kegen: *Waiting for everyone to gear up. Troy, Charity, Sammi and Quin are going to take up the first group.*

Marlowe: *You aren't jumping?*

Kegen: *Nope. There are only a couple people so I'm not needed. Wish you were out here with me so I could show you around.*

Marlowe: *That would be nice. Will I see you tonight?*

Kegen snorted loudly, drawing some curious glances. He ignored them and focused back on his phone.

Kegen: *Of course. It's the highlight of my day.*

Marlowe: *Mine too.*

Kegen: *What time are you planning on being home? Maybe we can do something away from the house tonight.*

Marlowe: *Not sure. I want to be home by four at the latest. What about you?*

Kegen glanced at the large clock on the wall again. If they had three loads going up, allowing thirty minutes or so for each trip, he could be out of there and home around the same time as her.

Kegen: *I might be home around the same time as you if things go smoothly here. We should meet up. Your place at five? Give us both time to shake off the day.*

Marlowe: *It's a date. You know what you want to do?*

Kegen: *You! But let's play it by ear. Just be prepared. I think something casual would work.*

Marlowe: *Crap, I have to go. Love the plan. See you later.*

Kegen stood, slipped his phone in his pocket and walked to Quin's office where Rev was still sitting.

"Hey, you doing okay?"

Rev glanced over his shoulder at Kegen before turning back to the computer. "Yeah. I'm bored as hell."

Kegen noticed Rev searching through a medical directory on the hospital's website. "What are you doing? Did you lose the number for one of the nurses doting on you the other day?"

Rev grumbled under his breath. "No. She didn't give me her number."

Kegen's eyebrows shot up. "What? A woman who didn't fall at your feet? I think your charm is slipping."

Rev snorted and clicked on another page. "No one could charm that woman."

"You've finally met your match, haven't you?"

"I just need her damn number to see if she can email me those dumb stretches and flexibility exercises. I lost the sheet with the ones she told me to do. What's everyone up to?"

Kegen looked out the glass window at the remaining four jumpers talking excitedly. "First load just went up." He turned his head back to his brother. "So, when do you want to get out of here and do you need me to babysit your ass tonight?"

Rev shot him the middle finger. "I'll be ready whenever you are. I don't need you around tonight either. Charity is coming over to entertain me."

"Jesus, you don't quit. Don't fuck up with her. We need her to keep working here."

"I'm not going to screw her. We're just friends who like to flirt. She's bringing me dinner and we're going to watch horror flicks all night. Her boyfriend is out of town. And before you ask. Yes, I know him. No, I'm not trying to take his girlfriend. The guy is some Special Forces dude and would probably kill me and hide my body where no one would ever find it."

"Good to know. I won't be around tonight, so enjoy your movies and popcorn."

"You finally going to take Marlowe out now that Mom and Dad have relinquished the house?"

"Yeah. Not sure what we're going to do yet, but it would be nice not to have to rush off back home because my parents are peeking out the window watching us."

Rev chuckled. "That was pretty damn funny. Mom wanted to go over with you and meet her. You were lucky Dad convinced her not to."

"Yeah, it probably helped that Dad met her already."

Rev turned toward him, studying him with a seriousness that rarely graced his twin's face. "You're pretty serious about Marlowe, aren't you?"

Kegen leaned back on the doorframe. "Yeah. Just being around her makes me happy. We could sit around watching TV all damn day and not have sex once and I would be content."

Rev looked at Kegen with mock horror on his face. "That right there must tell you something. You're actually taking the time to get to know the woman. I never thought I would see the day."

Kegen shrugged. He didn't think he would ever see that day either. He'd take it though. He didn't think these kinds of feelings would come around again.

Noises from behind Kegen forced him to turn around. The first group of jumpers were walking back into the hanger, followed by Quin and crew. Looking over his shoulder, he said to Rev, "As soon as they're all done, we'll leave. I'm sure Quin will understand you needing to get home to rest. You know, since you're the baby and need special care."

Kegen heard Rev call him an asshole as Kegen walked to join Quin. He would double check the next load's harnesses while the crew got their next tandem rig on. He could repack the chutes while they were in the air and get them put away. The quicker things got done on the ground, the quicker they could all get out of there.

Rev hobbled out of the office to stand next to him. "You're an asshole."

"I heard you the first time."

"Yeah, well…whatever." Rev made his way over to the lounge area, throwing himself down on the couch. He picked up the video game controller and soon the sounds of gunfire and air strikes filled the hanger.

Two hours later, around four o'clock, Kegen was pulling away from the Chute Shack with a grumpy Rev in tow. It would take them thirty minutes to get home. Ten minutes to get cleaned up. Allowing for twenty minutes of pacing and planning what the hell he and Marlowe were going to do.

He was pretty sure knocking on her door then dragging her to bed wasn't the answer. He promised her a date.

"What about the Wine Bar?" He didn't really say it to get an answer from his brother; it was more to think through what he wanted to do.

"What about it?"

"Taking Marlowe there. For dinner."

Kegen saw Rev shake his head out of the corner of his eye. "She goes there all of the time. It's right next to Whispers. I've heard they do lunches and wine breaks there."

"Damn. I wanted some place nice and that's the only one I can think of. Going to my usual is out of the question. Hank's is not the atmosphere I'm looking for."

"She'd probably like it though. I swear there's a wild child in her."

"Yeah, she probably would, but that isn't a date kind of place."

"It is if you're looking to get laid."

"I'm not looking to get laid." *Yeah, right!*

"You're lying to yourself if you think that. You've been dying to get in her pants for a week. This is your first actual chance without fear of something happening or someone interrupting. You can't tell me you weren't tempted to stay the night with her while Mom and Dad were staying with us. I know our damn couch isn't *that* comfortable."

"It wasn't, but there was no way in hell I wanted them to know what I was doing. It was bad enough dad caught me trying to kiss her."

Rev hooted. "That must have been a sight."

Kegen chuckled along with his brother. It had been a sight and a nasty reminder that he needed to be on his best behavior. Teasing and third degrees were not on his radar.

Rev snapped his fingers. "How about that place?" He pointed to a building a little ways in front of them. It was a new restaurant halfway between their house and the Chute Shack.

"It's finally open?"

"Yeah, Charity was telling me about it earlier. Her boyfriend took her there a week ago. Said it was very romantic and cozy."

"Good food?"

Rev shrugged. "Steaks, fish, and pastas. Not too expensive but enough to make you feel like you were making an effort I guess."

That's when it hit Kegen. He could take Marlowe to the new restaurant then out to the Shack. No one would be there. He'd be able to show her his workplace, their pride and joy, and quite possibly seduce her under the stars.

A grin kicked up the corner of his mouth. "Perfect."

Rev reclined his seat as far as it could go. He pulled his baseball cap over his eyes and crossed his arms over his chest. "You can thank me later, cause you know I just got you laid."

"Asshole."

Chapter Thirteen

Marlowe opened her front door to a grinning Kegen, and she had to do a double take. Her eyes traveled from the top of his slicked back hair, over his handsome face and down his impeccably dressed body. He wore a black sports coat, a white button up shirt, crisp dark blue jeans and a beautiful pair of shiny black slip on shoes with a metal buckle peeking out. She immediately felt underdressed.

"Change in plans," he said leaning in for a kiss.

She licked her bottom lip, craving more of his taste. "I see this." She looked down at her outfit. He had said casual earlier, so she threw on a pair of tan Capri pants and a black t-shirt. She was definitely underdressed.

"Go change baby. I'll wait." He stepped inside and shut the door behind him.

Marlowe rushed back to her bedroom slamming the door shut so she could indulge in a small panic attack without him watching. He looked so damn delectable she couldn't think straight.

A knock on the door had her jumping away from it. "You okay?" The smooth timber of his voice reached through the door like a caress.

She shuddered and moved toward her closet. "I'm fine. Just a little thrown by the change in outfit. You know it takes time to pick the perfect outfit, right? I wasn't expecting anything fancy."

"I wouldn't say fancy, just nice. You don't have to get changed if you don't want to. You're beautiful regardless of what you wear."

There was the charming guy she adored. Not that he wasn't charming all of the other times he was near, even when he was being a little overbearing and demanding.

"I'll be out in a moment. Have a seat or grab a drink." She waited until she heard him walk away.

Marlowe had been looking forward to the date since they made the plan. It was the first time in too long where they didn't need to worry about being interrupted. No employees or phone calls interrupting. No parents looking on to see what was going to happen, if anything. No more feeling like a lovesick girl with her first crush on the cute boy next-door. Well, that might not go away. Even as she pulled the strapless A-line, Princess silhouette black dress out of her closet, she still felt the bundle of nerves roiling in her tummy.

She quickly shucked her Capri's, panties, t-shirt, and bra before pulling out a sexy black lacy Bandeau bra top with lace-up front and matching thong from one of her overstuffed dresser drawers.

It was only fair that she knock his socks off as much as he'd done to her. He cleaned up well for an extreme sports junkie who favored cargo shorts or jeans and t-shirts.

Slipping on her new outfit, Marlowe made a quick stop into the bathroom, brushing her hair and applying a quick smoky look to her eyes. A dab of red lipstick and she was ready to go. A dash back into her closet where she pulled out her small black clutch and grabbed her sexiest black heels. She slid them on and took a deep breath to calm her insides.

Marlowe opened her door and went out into the living room. Kegen was leaning against the island in the kitchen. His hands were stuffed in his pockets and when he looked up, she swore she could feel the heat blazing in his eyes, as he looked her up and down.

He let out a low whistle and sauntered toward. "Damn baby, you look good."

"Thanks," she breathed out huskily. "I just wanted to look as good as you."

"Better. You will always look better than me." He ran his hands over her shoulders and down her arms until he captured her fingers with his. "So fucking soft."

Kegen pulled her toward him, keeping their fingers twined. He kissed her lips, slowly, gently, seductively until she thought she would melt into a puddle at his feet. Her pussy tingled. Her nipples tightened. Her body screamed *let me at him*. Sadly, he stepped away far too soon.

"Let's go eat. I have something special planned for later."

"I can think of something special to do right now."

Kegen laughed and tugged on her hand. With a sigh of resignation, she followed behind him. He stopped them at the front door. "You have keys and a coat? It might get chilly."

"Give me a sec." Opening the coat closet, she pulled out a knee length black coat with faux fur lining the cuffs and collar. It should keep her plenty warm if just being next to the man didn't do it on its own.

She transferred the necessary items like her wallet and keys into her clutch and was ready to go. When she went to slip on her coat, Kegen was there helping her out.

"I hope you don't mind riding in my truck." He glanced down at her feet quickly before looking at her face again.

"Nope. I'll have no problem climbing in and if I do, I'm sure you'll be there to help. Where are we going to dinner anyway? I don't think you ever told me."

"I didn't. It's a surprise. I just want you to sit back and relax."

Marlowe laughed lightly. "That I can do."

Kegen opened the front door, ushered Marlowe out and waited for her to lock up. He held out his arm, allowing her to slip her hand around his bicep. Something that sent shivers down her spine.

Forty minutes later, they pulled up in front of Adriana's. Kegen rounded the front of the truck, opening her door. Once she climbed down from the truck with Kegen's help, cause that damn thing was huge, they walked inside.

They were hit in the face by the aroma of grilled steaks and Italian spices. Marlowe's stomach grumbled. Kegen's looked down at her and grinned.

"I know what you mean. I'm starving."

"I hope this place is good," she said as she pressed her palm to her growling stomach. Appetizers were going to be called for and quick.

"Charity told Rev this place was good."

The hostess approached them before Marlowe could ask who Charity was. It was the second time he had mentioned her, so she assumed they worked together. "We're about to find out."

They followed the hostess to a booth against one of the walls. It offered a bit of privacy, but not so much as to get away with doing anything naughty. Unless, of course, you were into a bit of exhibitionism, which Marlowe wasn't— but for him she might.

Kegen helped Marlowe out of her coat and hung it on the hook mounted at the end of their booth before taking a seat across from her.

The waitress promptly showed up, ogling Kegen and ignoring Marlowe. Not that she really cared. Kegen didn't give the woman the attention she was desperately trying to get and quickly ordered them drinks and an appetizer.

Marlowe sipped the water the waitress sat down in front of her. "How did your day end up going?"

"Not bad. The jumps were good. The clients all took home video footage and pictures on DVD's. Nice little extra for the business. Rev had to do the editing since he wasn't much help doing anything else."

"The poor guy. He must have been bored out of his mind."

Kegen chuckled, a little half smile lifting the corner of his mouth. "Yeah. Bored is putting it mildly. I swear he ran to the truck when I told him I was ready to go. How did your day go? Anything exciting happen in the lingerie world?"

"Nope. It was a straightforward, non-shipment day for us. I have everything set up for the new lines coming in. Steph is going to look over the books and finances for me over the weekend. And the problem I had to get off the phone for wasn't really a problem."

"That's good. What do you have planned for the weekend?"

"I thought I would play it by ear. See how tonight went and maybe, if you're not busy, we could spend the weekend in bed at my place."

Kegen's eyes opened wide, surprise washing over his face. It quickly morphed into a wicked grin. Reaching out, he picked up her hand, running his fingers over her knuckles and between each finger. "I think that can be arranged. I might have to check on Rev once or twice, but I'm all about keeping you in bed for as long as possible."

The waitress showed up then with his beer, her glass of wine and gooey, cheesy sticks. Marlowe's stomach growled. She picked up a cheese stick, dipped it in the marinara sauce and wolfed it down before Kegen could say thank you to the waitress.

"You hungry there, babe?" Amusement twinkled in his eyes.

Marlowe moaned as she picked up another stick and ate it just as quickly.

"Why don't we order our meals," Kegen said. She nodded and he ordered; chicken fettuccini for him, chicken and mushroom cannelloni for her.

They didn't have to wait long for the meals to arrive. They talked about little things while waiting. Marlowe had another glass of wine. Kegen declined any more beer since he was driving.

An hour after they had gotten to the restaurant, they were leaving. Stomachs full and smiles on their faces.

Kegen helped her slip her coat on and escorted her to the truck. At the door, he crowded her against it before kissing her. Tucking his hands behind her, she thought he was pulling her in to get closer.

How wrong she was.

She felt the handle of the door as he pulled it open. Stepping back Kegen pulled her with him, then he turned her with gentle pressure on her lower back and helped her in.

"I've got a surprise for you. Something I hope you'll like." He brushed a kiss across her lips then shut the door.

Marlowe was sure she would like anything he did for her.

Chapter Fourteen

Kegen settled on the bench outside the hanger and just watched. Soft country music poured out of the open hanger doors along with some light. Just enough to see the ground and the area around them. Marlowe swayed to the music in front of him as she stared up at the stars filling the night sky.

"This is beautiful, Kegen," she breathed out. The sound sending goose bumps over his skin. It was soft, light and filled with wonder.

"I agree." Except he wasn't staring at the sky. He was staring at her. The smile lighting her face. The dreamy look in her eyes. He would be perfectly happy sitting right there and watching her forever.

He was in love with the woman. No doubt about it. No matter how little time they had been able to squirrel away together. No matter how much there was still left to learn about her. He was in love with her.

He looked forward to seeing her every day. Talking to her every day. He could envision moving in with her. Loving her until death parted them. If she walked up to him right now and said let's get married, he would find the nearest judge and get it done. He would make her his so quickly she wouldn't get the chance to second-guess what she was thinking.

Marlowe turned back toward him and came forward. "Thank you for bringing me out here. It was exactly what I needed after this week. It's also nice to get to spend some time with you."

Kegen pushed off the bench. He laced their fingers together before pulling her flush against his body and wrapping an arm around her waist. His heart beat wildly in his chest when she snuggled up close to him, laying her head and hand on his chest.

They swayed to the music drifting over them. He got lost in the feel of her body against his. The sweet curves of her breasts pressed into his chest. Her slim hand stroking over his shirt-covered flesh. Her head tucked beneath his chin. She was perfect. Delicate and strong. Smart and sassy.

"You know I could get used to this."

"What? Dancing out under the stars? It is rather nice."

"I meant having you in my arms. I could definitely get used to having you in my arms all of the time."

Marlowe tilted her head back and looked into his face. "I'd like that Kegen."

"What would you think about me moving in with you?" The words burst from his mouth. It wasn't that he hadn't thought about it before, but they still had a ways to go just dating each other. It felt right though. Being with her. Having her in his arms, in his life. He couldn't imagine finding someone else that fit him like she did.

Marlowe's head jerked back at his words. "Move in?"

"Yeah. I'm in love with you, Marlowe. I want to build a life with you and start it now. I don't see why we shouldn't move in together."

Marlowe laughed and Kegen didn't know if that was a good thing or not. "Not the reaction I was expecting."

"Laurel said when a Ferris boy finds something he wants, he goes for it."

Kegen grinned. "That's true. I don't want to waste any more time. We get along great. I'm definitely attracted to you."

"It's a good thing I'm attracted to you too then."

Kegen leaned in for a kiss, brushing his lips quickly against hers. "Yeah. Definitely a good thing. So what do you say?"

Marlowe leaned back against his chest and started them swaying again. He hadn't realized they had stopped.

She was quiet for what felt like minutes. Long, nerve-wracking minutes during which his mind had run off in a million directions. He was beginning to think this was her way of telling him no when she finally spoke. "Move in with me."

His mouth lifted in a grin. "You won't regret it."

Marlowe chuckled. "Oh, I'm sure I'll question my sanity—a couple of times—but you're right. This thing between us feels right. I can't imagine being without you, Kegen."

"I feel the same." Kegen leaned in to kiss Marlowe's lips one more time before dragging her back into the hanger to make love to her.

That kiss, though it wasn't their first, was the start to a brand new life. Kegen knew it was going to be a great one too.

THE END

About Brandy Walker

As a teenager Brandy would spend time at her Nana and Papa's writing angst filled stories of unrequited love. All revolving around whatever cute boy she had a crush on at the time. The stories, which no longer exist, were a way to get out the emotions bottled up inside. After a time her interests changed and writing got left behind.

After rediscovering her love of reading, romance to be specific, story ideas starting popping up in her head. With some prodding from her friends she decided to try her hand at writing romance and has written around ten stories in various states of completion. With a plan in place she's hoping to bring more of her stories to life.

Brandy is a Navy brat, prior enlisted Army, current Army wife, and mom. She lives in Washington State with her husband of 18 years, three kids and one dog.

email | brandy@brandywalker.net
Website | www.brandywalker.net
Twitter | www.twitter.com/Brandy_W
Facebook | www.facebook.com/brandywalkerfanpage

Tiger Nip Series

Craving More, Book One
TEZ Publishing

Corrine Hart is ready for a few days off for rest and relaxation. At the top of her to-do list is spending as much time as possible in tiger form and doing her best to banish all thoughts of the mysterious *Hunky Cupcake Guy* who spent the last two weeks driving her libido insane.

Jett Montgomery-Murphy just wants to know if the tasty treats that keep showing up at work are the same ones his best friend used to get while they were in college. a trip to *Sweet Confections* confirms what he thought and brings him in close contact with the one woman he's secretly lusted after for years, his best friend's sister Corrine.

A late night tryst leads to two tigers finding their mates and two humans unsure what to do next. Add in an overbearing brother, a best friend with her own drama, and a crazy ex-girlfriend that has a checkered past and you have a recipe for disaster.

Will Corrine and Jett be able to overcome the unexpected obstacles on their way to falling in love? Or will they throw in the towel before the relationship even gets off the ground?

What happens when you find yourself craving more....

Please enjoy this excerpt from Chapter One.

Corrine Hart ambled up the slope behind her sprawling two-story home. The rush of endorphins from the evening run settled in her system, sending pinpricks of sensation along her skin, the hairs lifting on the back of her neck. It was a feeling she would never tire of. The only thing that would have made it better was if her best friend in the entire world had been running next to her, hanging out like they usually did on a quiet Friday night. De-stressing from their hectic workweek before starting it all over again.

Sadly, her friend had been summoned home, and one thing MJ and Corrine never did was disobey their parents. Family was number one in both their lives.

In all honesty, it was probably best MJ wouldn't be around the next couple of days. Corrine's twin brother, Sampson, called earlier in the day and announced he would be there in the morning. Corrine wasn't in the mood to deal with the chemistry that always vibrated between the two of them. Not that MJ or Sam would ever admit to the attraction, and it didn't help that her friend couldn't say a single nice thing to Sam, or that he either acted oblivious to her presence or teased her unmercifully. It was always one extreme or the other. Never a happy medium.

Yeah, it was better this way. She was all for *less* stress right now. In an unprecedented move, she decided to shut the bakery down for the long weekend and take some much-needed time for herself.

Letting out a snort, Corrine plopped down in the grass and stretched her limbs before settling into the soothing task of grooming her front right paw. With each swipe of her tongue; her best friend, brother, the bakery, and every other nagging thought and task drifted from her mind.

Minutes passed by in complete silence, the repetitive motion calming her frazzled nerves. Eventually there was nothing left to groom and Corrine was finally able to enjoy the scenery. Off to the right, she could just make out the fuzzy shape of her neighbor's home in the distance. Close enough if there was trouble, still far enough away as to not disturb him. A look to the left, and the wooded area came to life as a warm breeze wound its way through the trees; limbs swaying and beckoning her to come play.

This was why she moved to Cascade, Colorado. The peace and quite of the woods mixed with a homey midtown feel. Open spaces mingling with shops galore. What every female shifter could ask for.

Corrine rolled onto her side, resting her head on the cool grass. Eyes closed, muscles relaxed she was almost asleep when the image of a man flashed into her head.

Short brown hair she ached to run her fingers through. Golden flecked nut-brown eyes that melted her insides when they locked onto her. Plus there was his sexy as sin smile that crooked up on one side, drawing attention to his full lower lip.

A purr rolled from her throat as she imagined him skimming his lips over her body. Stopping at her aching breasts for excruciating seconds before gliding lower.

At over six-feet tall, the mystery man was built like a hard-edged linebacker: broad shoulders, thick muscular arms and legs, and she'd bet the bakery he had abs of steel. It would take her days to kiss and explore every inch of his sun-kissed skin. Days she would happily give up to do just that.

She was dying to find out if he tasted as good as he smelled. Even now, when she took a deep breath, she could swear she smelled his rich, spicy musk. It had to be from her run-in with him earlier in the day and the lingering memories dancing through her head.

He visited the bakery in the flesh during the day and invaded her dreams at night. She was never able to get him out of her thoughts. Not that she tried very hard. She was more than happy to let him worship her body, if only in her imagination.

He was the kind of guy she fantasized about meeting and falling in love with. Too bad any time he was near, her knees went weak and her tongue refused to work. Not to mention the most she got out of him was a wink and a smile. For two weeks she had been a frustrated bundle of nerves on the verge of snapping. No amount of masturbation would make the ache for him go away, and damn it all—she tried her best to make that happen. She probably needed to replace the batteries in her favorite vibrator—again.

Claiming More, Book 2
TEZ Publishing

Sampson Hart has known **Mary Jane Poppy** for ten years. She's his sister's best friend, business partner, and has had a crush on Sam for years. When the mating pull hits him, he's ready to claim her as his own. Given their history, it should be simple. Right?

MJ has loved Sam since she was fifteen. But being a hybrid, she's been told all her life she won't have a mate. When Sam proclaims she belongs to him, she doesn't believe it; the mating pull isn't there, and Sam isn't meant to be hers.

Running back home to escape the love she feels for Sam, MJ agrees to become the companion of a man who lost his mate and has three young children to raise. It is the only way to set Sam free to find the one he is truly meant to be with.

Will Sam be claiming more or will the one he desires most find comfort in the arms of another?

Dallas & Kacie : Tiger Bite, Book 2.5
TEZ Publishing

It's the holiday season and **Kacie Cook** is counting down the hours until its time to close up *Sweet Confections*. Not that she had any great plans for the week the bakery is closed. She won't be seeing her family—yet again, and all of her friends are too busy. All she had planned is a little rest and relaxation. That is until the last customer of the night walks in. Could he be the one to bring some holiday cheer and possibly change her life forever?

The Tiger Bite is a short story featuring Kacie Cook, an employee at Sweet confection, and Dallas Andersen, the younger brother of Devon Andersen who appears in Claiming More.

If you're just looking for something to give you a glimpse of my Tiger Nip world then this is a good place to start, though I feel the books should be read in order to get the most enjoyment out of it.

Decadent ROAR
Decadent Publishing

Coming November 2014

About Decadent ROAR

The tales in Decadent Roar explore college life and beyond from the shapeshifter or were-shifter's point of view. What's it like to be away from the pack? What freedoms can be explored? What dangers lurk? Do you pledge a fraternity? What about a sorority? Does this college happen to have a shifter-only spot on Greek row? Through parties to mid-terms, to discovering who they are, characters in a Decadent Roar tale will take you on a journey through college love, the ups and the downs, and what happens when everything you thought you knew turns out to be even more difficult than you would have believed?

Shifted Plans
Shifter U

Blurb:
(Subject to tweaking)

Avery Hillman has one year of college left and once it's over she has plans, BIG plan. A job managing her family's medical practice, an apartment of her own, and a new life where she's the one in charge. No hovering family, no annoying siblings, and no mate to have to divide her time to be with.

Declan Weller has one more class to finish. One more thing he can cross off his ten-year plan. Once that is done he can transfer to the new job waiting for him and his new life. He isn't looking for his mate and as far as he's concerned, finding her can wait another two years.

The Fates have a plan of their own. One that includes throwing Avery and Declan in each other's path. It's high time those two found each other and learn the most important thing of all…sometimes plans need to shift.

Other Books by Brandy Walker

Tiger Nip
Craving More, Book One
Claiming More, Book 2
Dallas & Kacie: Tiger Bite, Book 2.5

Box Set
Sinfully Supernatural Contains Craving More

Freefall
Caught in the Moment
Fly Guy Next Door

Shifter U
Shifted Plans, Book One
Decadent ROAR, NA Paranormal
Coming Nov 2015 from *Decadent Publishing*

Future Books/Series
Finding More, Tiger Nip, Book 3 - TBD
Giving More, Tiger Nip, Book 4 - TBD
Seeing More, Tiger Nip, Book 5 - TBD

Captured by Color, Freefall, Book 3 - TBD
Revving Her Engine, Freefall, Book 4 - TBD
Spinning Out of Control, Freefall, Book 5 - TBD

Praetorian Guards Series - TBD
Mystic Zodiac Series - Starting Jan 2015

MYSTIC ZODIAC SERIES

Starting January 2015
One book each month

January - *Angel - Thane*

February - *Goddess / God - Parvati*

March - *Shifter - Gideon*

April - *Nymph - Lisa*

May - *Fae / Faerie - Celeste*

June - *Witch - Willow*

July - *Siren - Amber*

August - *Dragon - Adrian*

September - *Djinn - Colby*

October - *Vampire - Lucas*

November - *Spirit - Mace*

December - *Demon - Falcon*

www.brandywalker.net/bookshelf/mysticzodiac
www.facebook.com/mysticzodiacseries

www.ingramcontent.com/pod-product-compliance
Lightning Source LLC
Chambersburg PA
CBHW030236180626
46810CB00008B/3162